Rainbow Goddess

A Journey Tale

by Cynthia C. Whitehouse

MOONTRESS PRESS

Dear Reader,

This book is a synthesis of several areas of my life.

I am an Image and Color consultant with a passion for watching the way light waves influence people's behavior. Although, as humans, our relationship with color can be studied abstractly (like our relationships with food and other matter), interacting with light can also be a personal and subjective matter.

The Mystical, the Magickal, the Unseen and the Waiting-to-be-Seen all intrigue me immensely. Learning to become aware of the energies around me tugs at my creative impulses. Time spent in interplay with these forces led my imagination down the winding path of the journey you are about to join.

As with all fiction, some of this adventure is based upon experience while much comes purely from fantasy.

The characters are completely fictional. They are not based on any real persons.

Bon Voyage.

Magically yours,

Cynthia Whitehouse

www.moontress.com

A Moontress Press Book
Published by Moontress Press, Marquette, MI, USA

Copyright © 2000 by Cynthia C. Whitehouse

Printed on 60% Recycled Paper

Library of Congress Card Number: 2001116019

ISBN 0-9701835-0-X

Acknowledgements

I would like to express my deepest thanks to all the talented, generous and perceptive people who participated in the birthing of this, my first novel.

Editorial thanks and kudos go to Elizabeth (Beth) Clifford for having the stamina to trudge though the first, rather rough draft and help me set off in a coherent and comfortable direction.

Heartfelt thanks to the readers who gave input, feedback, corrections and much needed encouragement during the lengthy process of the book's development, including: Julia Starzyk, Mary Jane Eustace, Jean-Marie Magnier and Eugene Whitehouse.

More thanks go to Angela Wennerberg for combing through the last of the tangles and to Michaeleen O'Sullivan for putting a shine on the final product.

To Terri Nash, who guided me through mornings and afternoons of energetic energy exploration, which helped free me to re-edit this book, thank you.

Thanks to Jeff Rhodes of Thomson-Shore for infinite patience.

Thank you, Joe Johnson of Johnson's Printing. You saved my cover.

For the many hours spent advising, consoling and assisting with technical snafus, I thank you and love you Ken Whitehouse.

Finally, thanks to Luke and Shannon for their patience during meals that were served late and times when my complete attention was not on them. Thanks for hugs when I need them and for the smiles that keep me going.

I love and appreciate each of you!

- C.W.

To my personal Rainbow God, Ken Whitehouse, the man who has painted my world with soft strokes of warm and cuddly colors when I needed them and with the brightest, most vivid hues of life when I craved them-for over twenty years.

In Order to Awaken,
*   You Have to Wake Up*

Sometimes,
A force:
The slam of a door,
The jar of an injury,
Hits us
And we leap
Out of slumber
Into the brisk rush
Of reality.

Often,
We strain
Against
The lull
Of a dream:
A muddled life-plane
Where we are not ourselves,
Before we awaken.

Then,
There are times
When we are
Simply
Called
To the table
To break
Our reality fast.

Contents

Prologue

In the liquidy lull of a forever dream, one that returns again and again, she comes to me whispering, always whispering, "It is time, Karina, it is time."

I cover my face, fighting not to look into her eyes. Her eyes, as bottomless as the depths of space, as knowing as the eternal flow of creation, eyes that see everything and in-a-flash will show it to you, if you're not careful. I've looked into them before and wished that I hadn't.

I desperately want to not look. I want to go directly to that place in my mind that always welcomes me, if only I can find it. I try. Caught in the murky texture of the dream, I fail. Like my other dreams, the ones where someone is chasing me but I can't run, the ones where important words are written on a piece of paper, but I can't read them, like my other dreams, this one controls me and I turn to look. As a magnet being dragged toward steel, my eyes draw to hers.

"No," it comes out feebly. "No," I say, but I look.

This time, what I see is different. Her eyes are warm and their energy is strong, pulsating. Maybe she isn't just a goddess, I think. Maybe she is all the gods and goddesses merged together. Maybe she is the creator of existence.

I look into her and see myself. It's as though her eyes have focused to become a screen for the movie of my life. Unwillingly, I fall into the film.

I see myself in a lavender dress decked with ribbons and lace. I am a golden haired little girl with green-brown eyes. A puppy named Misty is nipping at my knees. She jumps up and snatches a piece of ribbon, untying it and tugging it off me in the grip of her sharp little teeth. I am laughing. Standing on the porch, Momma, however, is not. I feel her disapproval move straight through me, and I tremble, becoming that child again.

The scene changes. Now I am an adolescent. My body is still petite, but strong like a gymnast's. My hair is browner than before, with golden highlights. My eyes are more challenging. This time I am late coming home from a date. Momma, again, is on the porch. The same look of disapproval stains her face. The same sense of foreboding takes hold in my gut.

I sit down in a rocking chair. A low afternoon sun warms the sky. I look down and catch the glint of a diamond reflecting off my finger. I remember I am married. I turn my hand and the sun catches the cut of the rock, splaying a rainbow onto the wall.

Momma is sitting in the rocker next to me. I could be imagining it, but I think that her face has softened. I think she is actually smiling.

I wake up sweating, knowing I should tell Momma about the dream, as I should have told her about all the others. I'm sure I could do it more easily, if I thought there was a chance she would really smile.

Chapter One - Red
Passion Pursued

Momma is in the kitchen with Auntie Connie and Gramma. They don't think I'm listening, but I can hear them.

"June, you have to be careful to watch her breathing," Auntie Connie says to Momma. "Remember what happened to Aunt Elena."

"Elena wasn't ready for the journey. She was too impatient to wait for the dream," says Gramma. "Karina will be fine."

Somehow I don't find Gramma's words very comforting. She doesn't know what's going on inside me. No one does, since I rarely talk about my problems. It seems the more people know how weak you are, the more they try to control you. And I don't need any help screwing up my life.

"Let's not forget what happened to poor cousin Cura," says Auntie Connie.

I know these stories, which is why I'm afraid of this journey. Aunt Elena died during her journey. Just stopped breathing for no known reason. Cura went crazy. She hasn't been able to find her way back to reality. Although everyone says she still might, it's been over ten years and no one really believes it.

"Karina is a strong girl. Always has been," Momma says. "Anyway, living without the dreams is like swimming in emptiness, and I won't let Karina spend her life like that."

Momma has used her "that settles that" tone and I know there will be no more discussion. Gramma and Auntie Connie are here for moral support and to cook and free up Momma's time so she can concentrate on me. Actually, being the oldest crone, Gramma is the Overseer. Momma is my Guide. But the journey is really for me. I want to try to remember that. It's my journey. Gramma and Auntie Connie will be here for the entire thirteen days the journey takes, chanting and singing strange songs much of the time.

Entering into the journey room, I sense a change in the atmosphere that makes me catch my breath. It's not just the circle Momma has formed, both for concentrating the magick and for protection from outside influences. It's not just the stratus cloud layers of incense hanging heavily, which cleanse and ready the air. It's not just the light that has dimmed to the glow of a candle's flame and the little circle of space just beyond it, creating a world separate from the glare of normal reality. It's not even the moan and lilt of the sounds coming from Momma as she invokes the Goddess' powers, urging her to release her insights into me, teaching me what Momma cannot. No, it's more than those things. It is the play of these elements as they skirt from and merge with each other in a way that seems sacredly tempting-even to me-that has me both seduced and frightened by the invitation of this journey.

I step forward and reach to hold the Crystal Goddess in my hands. She feels cool and heavy in my fingers. For just a flash, I think I see the statue's eyes focus. I feel her presence touch me, like the force of a stranger watching from across the room, only without the distance. A chill goes up my spine. The already wild thump in my chest steps up a beat.

"Karina," Momma says. "It's time to begin your preparations."

I don't want to begin. I'm not sure how I got into this, but I'm sure that it's not entirely my fault. I used to be sure I would never take the journey. I was secure in myself. Sure of what was right and who was wrong. Now all of that's a little hazy. I didn't get this way alone. By myself, I'd be okay. It's with other people that I have a problem. In general, I find people very difficult. It's not that I don't like them. Usually they're all right. It's just that they can twist you up inside. Momma says this is because I haven't taken the journey. The journey is supposed to enlighten me with dreams and visions of my inner self, to ground me in who I am. Personally, I have my doubts. As far as I can see, the process has no scientific basis.

Although I have to admit that science and I have parted ways on occasion, I admire, even covet the structure and the security of science. I want the order and clarity of science in my life. I just have trouble believing that the unexplainable doesn't exist, because if that is true, then my whole family and I are probably mad.

It gets worse, if the journey does really reveal my deepest self, I'm not sure that she is someone I'll want to know all that well. Then there's the Goddess herself. She comes to me at night and whispers strange yearnings. I resist her, but still she comes. I haven't told Mamma about all her visits. I hoped if Momma didn't know this, then she wouldn't force me to go to this place or time or reality that no one could explain.

But, the women in my family have always taken the journey, and so I am obliged.

Anyway, it so happens that, at this particular point in time, I have nothing better to do with my life. My divorce was recently finalized. My job has been downsized out of existence. And my friends are all hopelessly addicted to the illusion of health they get by spending most of their time at the gym.

Momma has seen this, and used it to persuade me that now is the time for my journey. Momma sees everything, so there is no use pretending that I have something better to do. Still, I'm scared.

I carefully set the Goddess back on her rainbow-colored mat. There is a tingling in my hands, like a little magnetic force, urging me to pick her back up. I rub my hands together, trying to erase the sensation. Statues of the Crystal Goddess have been fixtures in my family for as many generations as anyone can remember. Each woman in the family gets one when she has her first menstrual period. Then, we wait for the Goddess to visit us in a dream. Sometimes the Goddess visits early in life, sometimes later. Some say they never have the vision.

Momma says, "of course the Goddess has come to them, they've just ignored her." I was hoping the Goddess wouldn't visit me, but, naturally, she did. She came to me in all the wonder of her spectral colors, pulsing with the power of her endless vibrations and urging me to follow the torch of her trail. Urging me to follow her through some enchanted wonderland that could leave me strong and solid like Momma and Gramma or leave me lost forever like poor cousin Cura.

Now, there are people who think we are a family of Matriarchal Witches, but Momma says that we are Spirituals. All I know is that I had to learn an awful lot of rhymes and meditations to take this journey. When I ask Momma what the difference is between rhymes and meditations, and spells and incantations, she just wrinkles her nose. I think there's a lot she doesn't tell me because of my skepticism.

The first step toward journeying is taking The Bath. Momma has drawn the water and perfumed it with special rose oils. I also smell sage, lavender and a trace of gardenia. The scent is slightly intoxicating. The water is hot against my skin. Sinking into its heat, I feel a welcome refuge. The bath is a symbolic cleansing of my worldly problems and attachments. The roses are supposed to reflect the "thorns-go-with-beauty" theory everyone seems to have bought into. Momma says it's immature and naive of me to think this isn't true. I disagree with her, silently. Silently only because we have had this discussion before.

I say, "Beauty can stand on its own. It doesn't need thorns to bring it out."

She says, "It's all about balance, Karina. Light is the other side of darkness. Without darkness there would be no shadows. No shadows, no forms. No forms, no way to even define beauty, but especially no beauty."

Then I say, "If there was no division of light and dark, then wouldn't the result be nothingness? And isn't that nothingness the ultimate nirvana that everyone is trying to achieve? So, by that definition, beauty without thorns is nirvana."

Then Momma says, "Karina, you don't understand balance. To learn about balance, you must take the journey."

It always comes down to that. I know nothing because I haven't taken the journey.

The journey through the Crystal Goddess is a sacred ritual of what Momma calls our "Timeless Coven." The Goddess has many names. Some call her Isis, some Diana, some Earth Mother, others Mary; it really doesn't matter. What matters to Momma is that there is an unbroken thread of honor and belief that has been sewn through the generations of our family coven. Each new generation has to demonstrate their trust in the Goddess by becoming vulnerable and opening themselves to the lessons of the journey. In return for this, the Goddess showers the believer with insights, protection and blessings. Momma says that I then bring the gifts I receive into the coven, that we are all connected in some way.

If I don't take this journey, I will be the only one in the coven's history to have broken the thread. I will miss out on the blessings and, I think, screw up the blessings for the rest of the coven, as far back in time as it goes. Of course, I could be wrong about this, but I'm afraid to ask, in case it's true.

It's a lot of pressure and a pretty confusing predicament for a girl who was raised half Spiritualist and half Catholic. At the time of their wedding, Momma promised Daddy she would send whatever children they might have to the Catholic Church. Momma honored her promise, even though Daddy left us long before I would have known the difference.

Nana, Daddy's Mom, told me once that Daddy had been enchanted with Momma in the beginning; but that, over time, he grew to find her Spiritualism "creepy." That's why he left.

"Did he find me creepy too?" I asked, only five years old at the time.

"No Honey," she said. "He just never looked back."

The heavy scent of frankincense, which Momma is burning in my journey room, is wafting into the bath and mingling with the rose oil mixture, creating a poignant aroma. It brings me back to the present. I know that it's time for me to dry off and begin the journey. Momma rubs me with a towel and wraps me in an ancient black silk robe. It's embroidered with pentagrams and crescents, stars and suns in brilliant reds and oranges, yellows, blues and every other color in the rainbow. We go into the journey room. Candles are lit and set in a circle and frankincense is burning in each corner. In the middle of the room I see the mat where I will sit. Next to it, the Crystal Goddess stands coolly on her rainbow mat, waiting to fly me, metaphysically, through her pulsating wavelengths of color, through the wonderful waltz of electromagnetic energies.

Most people don't think color waves influence us much, but they freak out completely about X-rays and microwaves. Momma says societies only acknowledge sensitivities based on what they think they can control. She also says my current insensitivity comes from the lack of control I exert over my life. I say I'm just not that interested in being sensitive to a world that is crass in its treatment of coexisting life. Momma smiles that smile that means she knows something I don't. She thinks I have created my own problems in this world. She thinks that I actually like conflict.

Which brings me to Jake. I wonder if I would be doing this if Jake and I were still together. The loss of our marriage is still fresh in my psyche. I can smell it like the lingering odor of freshly baked bread. Knowing that I will never taste it again is a constant frustration. Of course, living with him was a constant frustration too. He had changed so much since we'd first started dating. It was his job. Gradually the influence of police work seemed to seep into him and take over the more sensitive, gentler parts, the parts that I loved so much, the parts that touched something in me so deep that I felt he had dug a well from my soul into eternity. When we first got together, I was sure that he was my one, true soul mate, that I had known him for as many lifetimes as I had lived, and that I had always gone to bed at night cuddled into his all-encompassing spirit.

Then, one day I woke to find I was sleeping with a robotic cop. It got so that I began to think I could smell violence on him whenever he walked through the door. Smothered by his overprotective dictates and starved by his emotional stinginess, I just couldn't take it anymore. Jake would never have approved of this journey, which is partly why I agreed to it.

I breathe in the frankincense as though it were a joint of the great herb. This is my last chance to run and hide, but I know that if I do, I will have to hide from Momma forever. I take my seat and Momma takes hers.

"Remember to beware of the Fire Tunnel." Momma warns for the hundredth time. I'm still not sure of what the Fire Tunnel is, but I know that if I see it, I'm supposed to stop and wait.

"One more thing," Momma says. "Don't touch the tunnel walls."

"Touch fire walls? Of course not," I say.

"Any walls," she says.

Momma begins her chant... "Heiyo hay o yea o..." and I begin my rhyme to the color red:

Throbber of love
parts,
Sender of flames,
Sire of new
starts,
Form your arrows,
From hot metals
pound.
Fly them not straight,

"For true tales are
round.
Sear my facades.
Seek through me for
might.
Rescue chaos
Released in your
light.
Guide away heat.
Grow weak into
strong.
Permitting me leave,
Perchance I've stayed
long."

I pick up the Goddess and she is cool in my hands. Gradually, she becomes burning hot against my skin and I want to drop her. But I know I don't dare. I'm becoming dizzy. I think my eyes are still closed, but I can see that I'm standing in a dense, red fog. All around me is the color. It is so thick that I can't breathe. It's closing in around me. I remember Momma saying to listen for voices and follow them. Everything is silent.

Out of nowhere comes a low, steady voice. "Hi," it says. I want to hop on it and ride it out of here. I focus my eyes in its direction and a man appears.

He has red hair and ruddy skin. He looks as though he belongs here.

"I am your guide into this color," he says. "Take a deep breath. You're going to be fine." He's offering me his hand: the hand of a stranger.

I want to believe him. Something in me trusts him, though much of me does not. Still, I'm lost and he seems to know the way. Cursing my own weakness, I take his hand, thinking that I'm sure to regret this later. On principle I try not to let men lead me by the hand. But, since I am lost....

The red begins to fade into the background. It's still here, but not as oppressive. He walks me toward a fountain. As we get closer, I see that it's a structure made of glasses, crystal wineglasses. And the liquid bubbling through it is wine, red wine. The man steps over and removes two glasses, fills them from the fountain, and hands one to me. We toast.

"To your journey," he says.

He knows something about this. I have so many questions I want to ask him, but after I take the drink I become sleepy and have to lie down.

I'm in a restaurant. The menu says "The Villa Capri." I'm dining alone at a table. My mind is a little hazy and I'm not sure why. Everything in here is red, the carpets, the table clothes, the walls, the menu, but there are green plants. Thank God for green plants. The waiter comes over to take my order. God, he's handsome. He is my dream man. His eyes are like perfectly polished aquamarine stones. His hair is dark and has those natural waves women pay big money to duplicate. If it weren't so fluid, I'd swear his body was sculpted out of marble. His nametag reads "Jake." He looks really familiar, but I can't remember from where. Actually, I can't remember anything. I don't remember coming here, and I don't know why I'm eating alone.

"Good evening." He flashes me a smile and my heart begins to pound. "Our specials this evening are prime rib, served rare; spaghetti in marinara sauce and boiled lobster. May I take your order now?"

"I'll have a tossed salad, green, please. And the lobster, is it fresh?"

"Straight from the trap. Flown in on ice."

The trap, I think, the trap. I can't help but feel that his words hold some sort of warning.

That may be because I would believe anything he says. His smile is quite mesmerizing. Still, he looks out of place in this restaurant, but I don't care. I want him, and I'm not leaving without him.

I take off my sweater. It's really warm in here.

I eat the salad and some of the lobster, sucking the tendrils when he is looking, for effect.

"Will there be anything else?" Jake asks, handing me the check.

"A kiss." I don't know what made me say that. It's just that I feel a heat coming up inside me. It's giving me an oddly aggressive energy. But I like it. It makes me feel strong.

He looks around and suddenly I'm aware that there are other diners in the room. One table in particular looks like a party of mobsters. I don't know how I know this, but I feel they are violent.

"Why don't you give me your phone number?" Jake asks.

"I can't do that. I have a policy about strangers," I say stupidly. "Why don't you give me yours?"

He pauses for a moment then says, "555-1970. What about your name, do you give that to strangers?"

"Karina."

"I see." He says. "Well, Karina, I'm afraid you may have to take a rain check on that kiss."

I look in the direction his eyes have drifted and see a man whom I assume is the proprietor at the register. He is watching Jake, but not like a demanding employer watching an employee, more like a nervous conspirator.

"No," I say. "If you want me to leave, you will have to kiss me." This is pretty bold for me, but I'm feeling bold, if a bit edgy. The tension in the room seems to be building along with my expectation. Jake motions me to follow him toward the front of the restaurant. Then, stepping beside a sprawling fica plant, he pulls me into him and kisses me softly, parting my lips and sharing his moisture with mine. This is what I've wanted, but now I want more. When he releases me I am mush. The tension in the room is melting along with my lips.

"How about a last name?" he asks.

"Andrews," I lie, mostly out of habit, and I curse my friend Yollie for making me so paranoid. But, I have his number, so there's nothing to worry about.

I have been dialing the number he gave me for two days now and it is still being checked for trouble. My apartment is comfortable, but I've used way too much red in decorating. What could I have been thinking?

That's it! I'm calling my friend, Cindy, who works at the Telephone Company to have her look into this number. I can't think of anything but Jake and that kiss, and it's driving me crazy. I should have given him my number, or at least my real name.

The phone rings, then rings again.

"Hello."

"Karina? Hi. It's Cindy." I know it's Cindy. I can hear the chattering of voices behind her, operators speaking to their customers and to each other.

"Thanks for calling me back," I say. "I hated to bother you at work."

"No problem. I checked that number you gave me."

"And?"

"And I want you to promise you won't tell anyone that I told you this. Actually, you shouldn't even tell anyone that you know."

"Know what?" I'm trying not to let the frustration in my voice seep out, but I hear the edge developing.

"The number is a decoy, for the police. They use it if someone is trying to verify their ID, like when they are undercover."

"Undercover police? Well, that explains it."

"Explains what?"

"I've never been attracted to a waiter before. Not enough risk, I guess. Thanks, Cindy, I don't know how I'll ever repay you."

"Just don't tell anyone you got this from me. And be careful."

"I promise. Good-bye."

I know I have to go back to the restaurant, but I need a plan. Will I tell him that I know he is with the police? No. Then I would lose my advantage. I've found it's best to have an edge when you're dealing with men.

I pick up the phone and dial.

"Hello, Mark?"

"Yes. Karina?"

"Yeah, hi, Mark. I'm calling to see if you'd like to go to dinner with me at the Villa Capri. I have an passionate craving for their prime rib."

"Sure. Tonight?"

"Yeah, tonight's great."

"I'll pick you up at seven o'clock."

"All right. Seven o'clock. See you then."

This is really unfair of me. Mark has had a crush on me for a long time. He asked me out once. I said, "I don't want to ruin our friendship." Then he looked at me with those sweet, sad eyes and never mentioned it again. Still, sometimes, when he thinks I'm not looking, I see the way he watches me. It makes me sad. But, right now, I'm desperate. The passion that's driving me is speeding off course; and the strange part is I really don't care. Anyway, what's that cliché? "All's fair in love and war."

Mark picks me up in a red car and he is wearing a red sweater. I am wearing a sexy little red dress. "Designed for love," the salesgirl said.

The Villa is a red brick building with a large gold and black sign. There are two small windows in the front, and none in the rest of the building.

As I walk up the sidewalk leading into the building, I can feel that Jake is inside. I feel the pulse of his heartbeat. I hear the whisper of breath moving in and out of his body. I even smell the musk of his cologne, mixed with the heavy scents of garlic and cooking meat. It was a mistake to bring Mark. I know that now. But I'm committed. My body won't let me turn and leave, even though I know it's the sensible thing to do.

The host seats us and I notice that someone has removed all the green plants. Nothing else has changed, including the diners. That same table of violent men is sitting across the room. They're having spare ribs. Red sauce is dripping from their faces and fingers as they hold the meat to their mouths and gnaw at the bones. It's disturbing to see, but I can't turn away. One of them looks at me and winks his big, evil eye. That's enough. I can turn away now. Jake is coming to our table. I feel him behind me before I see him.

"Good evening," he says. "My name is Jake and I'll be your waiter tonight." As though I didn't know. As though every molecule in my body were not suspended in mid-air and doing a pirouette to celebrate his presence.

I look at him, and the blue in his eyes is the only thing in the room that isn't red. I smile, and he smiles back, politely. Mark orders the prime rib and so do I, although I'm not the least bit hungry for food.

The meal arrives while Mark's gone to make a phone call.

"You're number is out of order," I say to Jake.

"You don't exist." he says to me.

Touché. Well, at least I know he tried.

"I'm sorry about that," I say, "Reflex. Care to try again?"

"What will your friend think?"

"This is between us, isn't it?" I ask.

"It's never that simple, Karina. I think you know that."

Something in me snaps. "It's them," I say, "Isn't it?" Pointing to the mannerless group of men at the other end of the room. Immediately his demeanor changes. He becomes like a soldier on alert. I shouldn't have reminded him. I should have talked to him sweetly and kept him with me. Now he'll leave to fight his battles with the world and I'll be here alone, or with Mark. Either way I'll be lonely.

"Anderson," I say to him. "I'm in the book." And he is gone.

The phone has been ringing for a while, but I can't find it. I hate cellular phones, especially red ones. They blend with everything. Here it is.

"Hello."

"Karina. It's Jake. Are you all right?"

"Jake! Yeah. I'm hot, but I'm okay. I'm really glad you called. I've been thinking about you, a lot. Can you come over now? I'm going crazy without you."

"Karina, there's no time. You have to go now."

"To go? Go where? No. I can't leave now. I just found you. I have to have you."

There's a knock on the door. When I open it, it's Jake. But he's not coming in. He's offering me his hand, and I know that I have to take it. It's way too hot in here. He leads me down a long, narrow, red tunnel. The red of the tunnel is so bright and alive. I start to reach out to see what it's made of, but Jake grabs my hand. He shakes his head "no." The familiarity of that motion, that side-to-side swirling disapproval wrenches my gut back to another reality.

There is a white light at the end of the tunnel; I can hear Momma chanting.

I open my eyes to find Momma wiping my forehead with a cool cloth. The candles are merging together as one large flame. Everything else is blurry. The smell of frankincense is assaulting me. It's too strong. I begin to cough. Momma passes me some mint tea. It's like an elixir to my body. I feel it quench the fire in my throat. It even seems to help my nausea. I am back with Momma and without Jake. Just like real life. Of course, this is real life - or is it? I'm still pretty confused. Momma is caressing my hair, and somehow I know that this is what's real.

Momma looks at me for a long moment. "Do you want to talk about it?" she asks.

"Not now," I say. The feeling of loss is too fresh and I'm afraid I will cry. What did it all mean? I am so tired. "I just want to sleep," I tell Momma.

"Not yet," she says. "You have to stay awake for a while. If you go back to this dream now you may never wake up." I want to tell her that I really don't care, but I don't have the energy to fight her.

"What did the tunnel look like?" she asks.

"The tunnel?" I say. I've just lost Jake again and all she cares about is the tunnel? "Red. Everything. The restaurant was red. My apartment was red. The tunnel was red."

"Good," Momma says. "Would you like to go for a walk with me?"

I'm focusing better. I can see her clearly now. I can tell that she is as exhausted as I am. "No. I think I'll go alone," I say. She can stay here and rest. Anyway, I don't feel like talking to her just yet. Momma means well, but she has a judgmental streak in her. No matter what I do, I would have done it better if I had just done it her way.

Walking past my car, I'm tempted to get in and drive over to Jake's place. Then, I remember that we aren't friends anymore. What happened to us anyway? Did he really become such a bastard? Or was it I, wanting him to be everything, to be perfect? Of course he wanted the same of me. Strange how people like to love their gods but can't find much compassion for each other. When I first met Jake I thought he was perfect: A God. Actually, I didn't decide that he was human until after we were married. Boy, did he become human then.

As I pass a neighbor's house, a loud, guttural bark assaults my ears. I turn to see a huge German shepherd. Max. He's fenced in, but I still don't like his attitude. My head is clearing now. I am definitely not going to Jake's, although I may call him later. He did look really good in my "dream."

Gramma and Auntie Connie made pea soup, a large Caesar salad and homemade dill bread for late dinner. I'm suddenly ravenous.

After dinner Momma says I can go to sleep. "Tomorrow will be another big day," she says. "But don't forget to write in the journal."

❖ ❖ ❖

June 10

First Journal Entry: Red

>   *Momma told me to keep a journal of my journey. She says it will help me to keep the realities straight. She's going to keep one too, a Guide's journal, but I'm not allowed to read it until sometime later. When, I don't know. Everything has a reason with Momma. She just doesn't share them with me.*
>   *Well, here I go: It was different than I expected. I expected to know where I was. It's strange that I didn't recognize Jake, I mean, as MY Jake, even with his nametag on. And the other people, Mark and Cindy. I don't even know them. I'm wondering whether these are actual "spirits" who've come to help me on my journey, or whether the whole thing is a figment of my imagination. Maybe it's just my subconscious working overtime.*
>   *Either way, I'm stunned by how attracted I was to Jake, considering all the negative feelings I've had for him lately. I do understand my wanting to expose Jake as a fraud. That could certainly be my subconscious. I don't understand his rescuing me from the heat and protecting me from the tunnel walls. Jake rescues other people, not me.*
>   *I hope I don't spend this whole thirteen-day journey in a state of amnesia. I don't see how I can learn anything from this kind of trip. I'm worried about how much my emotions, the needs, the passion took over me. I was out of control. I wish I could have remembered that I was in the dream. I think I would have been able to be more objective if I could have just gained some distance. Next time, I'm going to try very hard to remember. K.*

I lay down, and I am so tired that I forget all about calling Jake.

✡ ✡ ✡

June 10

Guide's Journal, First Entry

Today was a day I've waited for a long time, the first day of Karina's journey. She wasn't prepared enough, despite my repeated warnings, but she's strong. She's always been a stubborn and passionate girl. I knew that she'd be okay in Red. She was. She has an affinity for passion. Although, I did see what I thought was a glimpse of desperation seep in through that armor of defense she puts on so well. If she doesn't recognize it, this may be a problem later.

I passed strength to her through dimensions, but she rejected me, and I had trouble cooling her down toward the end of the journey. I know she's depending on me to carry her through this, but she's going to have to open up so that I can reach her. Self-reliance can be a good thing, but without receptivity, it can be an obstacle. I have counseled her on balance more times than I can say. She refuses to look at the shadows in the light, or, maybe she is seeing the shadows and refusing the light. In either case, I wonder what she is afraid of. Whatever it is, we'll know soon enough. The Goddess shines her light brightly on weakness.

Karina still sees her taking this journey as a favor to me. I wish she understood the importance of it. Maybe then she'd spend a little more time trying to understand her place in the drama that's unfolding. Blessed be.

Chapter Two - Pink
Living Love

My body and senses softened and cleansed, I sit on my mat in the journey room. The smell of roses, lavender, gardenia and frankincense is penetrating my nostrils. Momma is wrapping the embroidered black robe around me again. I am more unsure than ever of why I am making this journey.

"Karina, you have to be careful not to stay so long this time," Momma says. "Just look for the lesson in the dream and take the tunnel back as soon as you've got it. Remember, the dream is the teacher."

"Really, Momma, I forget why I'm there when I'm in the dream. I forget who people are. I forget that it's even a dream. I'm really not sure that I'm meant for this."

"Of course you are meant for this! Everyone is meant for this. You are just luckier than most in that you were given the opportunity."

Well, I knew she wouldn't go for it, but it was worth a try.

My mind is resisting this experience, but my body betrays me. My senses are heightened and drawing me toward the Goddess Statue. The hairs on my skin are tingling, like little antennae searching for a connecting vibration. I am appalled at my physical being's willingness to feel the strangeness and light of another dimension. Maybe there is something besides flower essence in the aromas I've been inhaling. Or-a more appalling thought-maybe this is just my old escapist habit fulfilling itself.

"You just have to concentrate harder, Karina. And remember to mind the tunnel of fire," Momma brings me back with her admonishment.

"Yes, Momma."

Her warning of the fire tunnel reminds me of a lesson she gave me as a child. Momma was always showing me little "secrets," saying that someday they would have significance.

I was about six when Momma taught me about the hidden power of the sun's light. We were outside. We sat on the sidewalk. Momma had with her two objects made of glass. One was cut like a pyramid. The other was round with a handle.

"Pay attention," Momma said. She held the first object into the light and turned it until a beautiful rainbow appeared in the air. I was awestruck. "The light looks white but is actually made up of many colors. The lesson here, Karina, is that most things are not what they appear to be."

Momma took the round glass with the handle. She held it over a sheet of paper. We waited. I remember being impatient. Momma's concentration never wavered. Suddenly a little tiny spec in the center of the paper began to turn brown. Then it sparked. Fire began to burn in a circle, growing from that tiny spec until it engulfed the whole page. I studied Momma's face as she watched the paper burn. When it was gone, she looked me in the eyes and said, "There is power in the world beyond what you can see; harnessing it is another matter."

I didn't understand that lesson. But I never forgot it. Actually, I was afraid of what that power might be. I remember wondering whether it was the same power that touched me while I slept, waking me with its presence and hanging above me as I stared at the darkness. I told Momma about the unwelcome visits once.

"Of course there are other spirits sharing our space. If you don't want them in bed with you, just tell them to go away," she said. Living with a "Spiritualist" mother did not make for an easy childhood.

Momma is looking at me impatiently. I nod my head, and she begins her chant. I pick up the Goddess and begin my rhyme to the color pink:

*Toucher of moments
soft as the skies,
Deep as the forest,
true as good-byes.*

Rainbow Goddess: A Journey Tale

Giver of mornings,
good wine and bread
Sharer of comforts
quilting my bed.
Passer of penance.
Bringer of hope.
Changer of hues,
beige becomes taupe.
Find in the silent
subtlety core
Guidance for healing
inner wound war.
Remember, remember, remember..."

I'm in a cloud of pink cotton candy, except that it's not sticky like cotton candy. Well, maybe it's a little sticky in a humid sort of way. A young girl's voice calls out "Karina?" I look for but cannot see her. There is so much pink. Where did it all come from? I begin to feel a tugging on my skirt and she is there: a baby, a cute little blond baby girl, dressed all in pink, wearing a pink bonnet. No wonder I didn't see her.

"Come with me," she says, taking my hand. I am tickled that she is so cute. I want to play with her, but she keeps walking. We're going toward a lemonade stand. She seems to know the owner.

"Two pink, please, for me and my friend," she says, winking at the little boy as he pours. She hands me a paper cup and raises hers. "To your journey," she says. I toast with her and then she is gone.

Now I am at the edge of a large forest. There is a path leading in. Someone has planted pink astilbes all along the sides of it. They are in full bloom and their plumes brush my legs where the path narrows. The trees are both welcoming and protective. I feel safe here. I am happy just to be walking along this path. The Earthy scent of leaves decaying and being reborn fills me with a feeling of hope.

Then, off in the distance I hear a child's cry. It's a sad, whimpering cry. I start to walk faster, listening to make sure that I'm still walking toward it. The trees all look the same and the crying doesn't seem to be getting any closer, but I'm sure I haven't been walking in circles. I've lost track of time. It seems I've been walking for a long while now. Still, I can hear the whimpering off in the distance. Is the child lost? I'm pretty deep into the woods, but the pink astilbes still frame the trail. I find that reassuring. The child is still crying and I want desperately to find him or her.

Up ahead I see a large basket in the middle of the path. It's pink and there are pink blankets draping out of it. When I reach it and bend down, I see a baby: a brand new baby, maybe a few days old. The child is still crying in the background, but the baby is alone too. I don't know what to do. I look around for the mother. No mother would leave her baby alone in the woods. There must be something wrong. The baby's eyes are opening and she starts to cry. I pick her up and go to sit in a bench I spot just a few feet away. The bench is brand new, just like the baby. I begin to rock this sweet little bundle of helplessness, and she stops crying.

"You have the touch." I turn and see Jake standing behind me.

"Jake, what are you doing here?" I ask.

"What do you mean, what am I doing here? This is where we agreed to meet."

"We did? Never mind that. Look, Jake, I've found a baby."

He's laughing, now. Did I say something funny? "What is so funny?" I demand.

"You're funny. Finding a baby."

"Well, I don't think it's funny. Who would leave a baby alone in the woods?"

"No one left it alone in the woods," he says. "It's our baby."

"Our baby? How can that be?"

"You mean you don't remember? You and I made this baby, five years ago."

"Five years ago? But that was a miscarriage. The baby didn't live." I say.

"Apparently it did. You are holding onto it." He says.

The baby begins to cry and I can tell that she's hungry. I offer her my breast, and there's milk in it. She seems so satisfied, lying there, feeding on me. I want to whisper to her that she'll always be safe with me, but I know that's not true, since I have already lost her once. Instead, I whisper, "I love you."

"I love you too." Jake says. To me, or to the baby? I can't tell.

"What about the other child, the one I heard crying?" I ask.

"I didn't hear anything." Jake says.

But I know that I heard it. Maybe someone found him, or her. Though somehow I think it's a he. I can't say exactly why. I watch the baby as she suckles softly. For a moment, I am lost in her need, in the way she so honestly expresses and fills it. I wish that I could be that easy with life.

The baby finished her nursing. Now, I'm becoming anxious again.

"Let's go for a walk." I say to Jake. "I want to look for that other child." He gives me a funny look.

"Okay," he says. "It's your call. It's always your call, Karina."

I'm not sure why he said that, and I don't understand the look he's giving me.

"No. It's not," I say. "Not always. You are the one who always expects and demands. I am in no mood for this, Jake. Pick up the basket. Please," I say.

He is shaking his head at me, as if he can't believe something about me. This makes me angry.

"I don't want to put the baby down," I explain.

I don't know her name, but she looks like an angel to me, so I'll call her Angela.

"Her name is Angela," I say.

"I know." Jake says.

We move deeper into the woods, but the only sounds are rustling leaves and far off crows.

"Do you know where you're going?" Jake asks.

"No, I only know that he needs me," I say.

"What were you thinking of when you heard him last?" he asks.

"Nothing, really. I was just enjoying the feel of the woods. The leaves, their death and rebirth...that's what it was."

"Go back to that," he said.

He's right. My mind is so full of Angela. I can't think of anything else right now, but I try.

There is a fire burning ahead and the smoke is coming out in big, pink, billowy clouds. It smells like the sugar of burnt cotton candy. I step into it and I hear the cry. And music: I hear little, carnival merry-go-round music. Then I see him. The little boy is stuck on the merry-go-round and he can't get off. All of the other horses are pink; he's sitting on one that is black. I really want to help him.

"Please help me, Mommy," he says. I look around. I'm the only one there. Where did Jake go? Just when I really need him, he disappears. I set the baby down in some soft grass. I walk all around the merry-go-round, but I can't find the controls. They must be on the carousel. The boy is still crying, "Please help me, Mommy," and my heart is breaking. I'm going to have to jump on, but it's moving so fast.

I have chosen the pole I'm going to grab, and I watch as it goes around, timing its pace. It should be in front of me in ten seconds.

Five, four, three, two...

I'm on. I'm making my way to the child.

I put my arms around him and feel an instant connection to his soul. His crying has stopped and he is looking up at me, his eyes still red. "Why did you do it?" he asks me, and I know what he means.

"I was so young," I tell him. "And I had been doing drugs. I was afraid you would be, I don't know. Well, I was just afraid."

"I have missed you," he says.

"I've missed you too." I say. "You'll never know how sorry I am." Tears are rolling down my cheeks.

"It's okay, Mommy," he comforts me. "Some things just don't work out. You have to let me go now. I have other places to be."

"I'm sorry," I say. "I just missed you so. It's hard to let go."

"I can't be with you here, but my spirit is a part of you. You mourn for me as if my spirit was dead, but it's not. No one ever really dies, we just move to other places." God, he's a wise soul. And now I love him all the more.

"Will you visit me?" I ask.

"I am always with you, because you want me. Just don't think of me in sadness anymore, please," he says. "I am tired of this merry-go-round."

"I promise. I'm tired too." I say.

He kisses me and is gone: My little angel.

Angela! I remember my sweet baby, Angela. I look over and she is lifting from the grass, floating in air and I know another angel is carrying her. I want to grab her, but realize that I have to let her go too. I miss her, again. But no one is crying now. Not the child I left, nor the one who left me.

The little blond girl is back, smiling at me now and taking my hand. She is leading me through the pink cloud. I can feel her special, kindred spirit surrounding me, just as I can feel my Angel and Angela's. I close my eyes and the tunnel appears. Its walls are pink and thick, like the smoke I came through earlier, but the passage is clear. I walk into it. It seems to narrow a little ways ahead. I feel like I'm in a vein whose walls have become thick with built up cholesterol. I come to the narrowing. I turn sideways to squeeze myself through, trying to forget the touch of claustrophobia that is pumping up my adrenaline. The instant I think of it, I know I shouldn't have.

"I'm fine, I'm fine," I tell myself. My heart is pounding wildly. "Just breathe normally, Karina. Everything will be fine."

I close my eyes and slip through the narrowing. I open my eyes, afraid to look ahead. I see an opening not too far away. I breathe deeply. The air is thinner and lighter now. I start to walk quickly toward the opening. Jumping through the hole, I feel as though I'm falling up. Is it this world that is upside down? I wonder, or is it me?

I tilt my head back and focus to see Momma smiling at me. I'm able to smile back at her. I feel as though a great weight has been lifted from my shoulders. Actually, from my entire body. She holds me for a while, her motherness pressing close into my heart. We haven't had many moments like this, together and peaceful.

"What color was the tunnel?" Momma asks. Her voice is softer than usual.

"It was pink,"

"Good," she says.

"Momma," I say, "Are you glad that you had me? I mean, are you really glad? I know your life would've been really different without me."

"Karina, you don't have to ask me this. You know the answer."

What she means is that I should know that she loves me, and I guess I do. She's holding me closely, and I can feel her warmth. But still, I did need to ask. And I wish she would answer.

"Let's get something to drink," she says. "My mouth is dry." We walk into the kitchen together.

Momma pours me a glass of iced mint tea. Going down my throat, it feels like a mountain stream on a hot summer day.

"There was a telephone call for you while you were journeying," Gramma says. "It was Jake. Something about a cemetery plot."

The excitement I feel at hearing Jake phoned quickly turns to defensive resentment. Of course, the cemetery plots. Neither of us had remembered to list them as property in the divorce papers. Who thinks of cemetery plots as assets at twenty-nine? The only reason we have them at all is because of Momma. Momma is sure that one of the first things a new couple should buy together is their cemetery plots. "Knowing that you will be buried together gives a sense of grounding to your relationship," Momma said. It didn't help ours.

"He wants you to call him back," Gramma says.

"Karina, I didn't want to tell you this before you went journeying, but there's something you should know," Momma says. "Jake's mother died last night."

"Mother Calloway died?" The first thing that flashes in my mind is the face of the little girl in my dream. The way she looked and the way she winked. Mother Calloway always had that little glint in her eye and was famous for her left-eyed wink. Had she been visiting me from the "other world"? I have no idea how these things work. I wish I had spoken to her, Mother Calloway, that is. I've been so embarrassed over the break-up that I'd been avoiding her. I feel that hollow ache again, in that deep space in my heart where I hold all my regrets.

"Poor Jake." I say. "To lose your mother." I look at Momma and know that someday this will happen to me. "I'd better call him," I say.

My fingers tremble as I pick up the phone. I curse my own weakness. What is it that this man does to my insides? No, I don't want to analyze that.

"Hello," he says in a weary voice.

"Hi, Jake. It's Karina."

"I know your voice, Karina. Thanks for returning my call."

"Momma just told me about your mother. I'm sorry. What happened...if you want to talk about it?"

"Embolism. She died in her sleep." He says this like a detached, objective reporter so I know that he's having a really hard time dealing with it. "I called about the cemetery plots. Mom doesn't have one, and there's not much money for the funeral and all. I wanted to know if you would mind if I buried her in mine?"

"No, of course not. Actually, you can give her mine if you want to." I love Mother Calloway, but lying next to her forever is not how I envision my eternity. There's a silence on the other end of the line. Even though we are being cordial, it seems this willingness to give up our final resting spots makes the divorce more final than the court pronouncement did.

"Will it be okay if I go to the funeral?" I ask.

"Yeah. Mom would've liked that."

"Jake, I know you think of your mother as gone, but I really believe her spirit is still with us." I want to tell him about my journey and the children, but he will think I've lost my mind. I remember all the laughs we once had over the crazy women in my family. Jake was never comfortable with Momma's "sorcery" as he put it. I wonder what he would say if I tell him that he is in all my dreams. I used to tell him everything. Now my tongue plays dumb; and it's just as well.

"Jake, I'm sorry," I manage to say. "About your mother," I add quickly, before he gets the idea that I'm taking the blame for our entire relationship.

"Thanks," he says. "The funeral's tomorrow. Nine o'clock at St. Patrick's."

"Get some sleep." I say.

"Yeah, bye." The air in the phone is empty again, and so am I.

❖ ❖ ❖

June 11

Second Journal Entry: Pink

> *The dream-journey through pink touched my core at a depth I hoped I would never go to again. Without even realizing it, I had blocked some very sad memories from my mind. I'm not sorry now to have brought them back. The pain was oddly freeing. I think I understood the message of love and letting go. I recognized Jake this time. He was supportive in a*

way, but then vanished. His mother vanished in real life, like the guide in my dream. But then the guide came back. Jake didn't. Yet I will see him tomorrow. Then he and his mother will both be gone for me. I can't help wondering: will he be there in my next dream?

I'm more confused than ever about the connection between reality and the dream-states.

Meeting my babies and holding them could not have felt more real. On the other hand, I know all the feelings I experienced were buried deep inside me. Did it take the power of the resonating colors to excavate them? If it did, that's a pretty strong tool.

Which brings me to the Goddess. Who, exactly, is She? And how is it that a rhyme to Her spins me into a consciousness I know I could never have reached alone?

Momma might be able to help with this. She's pretty well tuned into the Goddess. I don't seem to be able to connect with either of them on my terms.

I never told Momma about the abortion. I doubt that now is the right time to start confessing. Helping me with the journey seems to take a lot of Momma's energy. I've always kept my distance from the Goddess, but this morning I found myself looking through Momma's books on Goddess history. Maybe I will do a little research. Maybe.

I feel a strong energy when I'm in the dream-state. It's not really threatening, exactly. Still, it's so powerful that it scares the heck out of me. K.

June 11

Guide's Journal, Second Entry

Karina's journey through Pink was successful. It was an emotionally costly dream, but she handled it well. She's still so closed that it was hard to tell whether she understood the message of love as a catalyst to finding her deeper spirit. She sometimes lives so superficially that I worry about the separation between her mind and her spirit. After all I've taught her, I don't think she can be unaware of the facade the physical world projects. Although, I have to admit, I spend so little time Earth-bound anymore that I can feel the distance between us growing. I try to keep myself near her, but the spirit side is so enticing and so comfortable. I find the physical plane more and more unattractive. I fear, if she doesn't come my way a little, we'll have no common ground left to work from.

I'm glad she finally dealt with her feelings of guilt about the abortion. She thinks I don't know, but she forgets that mothers know everything. Carrying the heavy emotions of abortion can be such a burden. I could see how it weighed her spirit down.

I can't tell if she understands the significance of Jake's coming and going. There's a lot about that relationship she doesn't understand. I hope she begins to see how entwined her spirit is with his. It's exciting to watch their energy when they're together. They meld and dance like one being. Neither of them even has the slightest clue to the uniqueness of their relationship. That amazes me. That they cannot keep a civil tongue with one another completely befuddles me. Karina fights for the independence that everyone else calls loneliness; and Jake fights to keep her from experiencing it. Of course, he has his own brand of loneliness. I don't know if even Karina can heal that.

I was hoping their relationship would not play so heavily in the progress of her journey. It's like Gramma says: "Thick cords left uncut will always tangle." Blessed be.

Morning came so early. It seems like I hardly slept. I know I had a lot of dreams, but I can't remember them. It took me a while to find a parking space at the church. The pews are full of people dressed in varying shades of black and gray. I am intensely aware of the brilliant colors of the flowers surrounding the casket, and of their contrast to the clothing of the mourners.

I want to say that we should be celebrating this woman's life, but I'm as sad as the rest of them. Mother Calloway was very special to me - mainly because she gave life to Jake Calloway, the man that I thought was my soul mate. I was grateful for that. Now my soul connection is gone, and so is its bearer. Big drops of salt water roll from the corners of my eyes. Forging a creek, they soon feel like a river traversing my face. I know I'm a mess.

Jake's back is to me, but I can read his pain in the rigidity of his shoulders. Not a muscle twitches; he is pulled so tightly into himself that I am afraid for the molecules inside him. All that pressure. I let myself think that, maybe, if I rub his shoulders just a little, I can give him some relief. The realization that I am still his wife, sitting behind him in the back of the church, slams me with guilt.

After Mother Calloway's body has left and the service has ended, I want to slip away without talking to anyone. I know that I look terrible, but it isn't other people's gazes I'm hiding from. I just can't listen to the rote banter of funeral chat right now. And I don't want to see the pain in Jake's face. If I get too close, I'm afraid I may end up in bed with him. The pain of feeling the distance between us when we are physically that near is more than I can stand right now. Though I know it's not polite to leave, I find my legs leading me quietly out the side door.

The day is clear and the air is fresh on my salty face. I am glad that the sun is shining for this burial. I look up to the sky, and send a wink to Mother Calloway, wherever she is.

Chapter Three - Orange
Controlling Chaos

I am getting used to the "roseincense," as I have come to think of it. Today, the fragrance is actually appealing, almost reassuring, the way the smell of garlic cooking in a sauce promises that your taste buds will be satisfied. I still would rather feast at home than in some faraway land.

One look at Momma tells me that this point is moot.

The Goddess statue is as heavy in my hands as my heart is in my chest.

"Karina," Momma says, "the magic of the journey comes from your ability to traverse in both worlds simultaneously. You have to bring your whole self and all your memory into each world."

"Exactly how do I do that?" I ask.

"You remember who you are and why you're there when you journey into the color-dream dimension. You bring your conscious self along." Momma gives me a sideways look. She asks, somewhere between testing and teasing me, "Do you think you can do that?"

"I'll try," I say.

"I'm here if you need me," Momma says. And then she nods.

I begin to recite my rhyming entrance into the Goddess's world, into the color orange.

> "Builder of structures,
> forces and foods,
> Bringer of reason
> balancing moods,
> Former of heart-rays

reaching the soul,
Focus my searching
lend it control.
Stirrer of motion,
energy's lift,
Feeder of questions,
show me your gift.
Remember, remember, remember..."

I've stepped into a place where the slamming of gallons of liquid-against-liquid drones in my ears. Beneath my feet, the ground is slippery. I'm in a cave of sorts. The liquid is running in front of me in big sheets of orange. It's a waterfall, and I am underneath it.

"Hello, Young Lady," comes the gravelly voice of an old man.

"Hi," I say, turning to see who has joined me.

"Welcome to the Irascible Orange," he says, dancing a slow, soft-shoe shuffle in front of the falls. He's dressed like a jester, wearing that silly hat with curved points jutting out of both sides of his head. He has on a roomy jumpsuit that is split vertically, orange on one side and gray on the other. It's hard for my eyes to focus on the whole image. I want to look to one side or the other.

He pulls two thin juice glasses out of nowhere and dips them into a small pool that acts as a temporary dam for a little of the raining liquid. He hands me one, "to your journey," he says.

From the saturating aroma of the cave, I taste what I know will be orange juice. It's as fresh as if I'd picked it right off the tree.

"Thank you." I say.

"Thank you for what?" I'm standing on the front of a stage in a very large theater. Glaring stage lights are shining down on me and I can't see who asked that, but I know it's not the old man.

"Never mind," I say, trying to get my bearings. At the back of the stage hang large, heavy, burnt-orange drapes. They're hiding the movement I can hear behind them. In front of the stage are rows of chairs rising up toward the doors. They are upholstered in the same burnt-orange as the curtains. There is the outline of a person sitting in one of the first rows.

"Well, can I have my set?" the outline is asking.

"You're set?" I ask.

"Yes, you are here to design the set for my play, aren't you?" He's a rather snide man, and I'm tempted to say "no" and leave, but I have no idea where to go.

"The play. Oh, yes, the play. What was the name of it again?" I ask.

"Two Thieves. Are you all right, Lady? I mean this isn't exactly your first job. I've seen your work before and it's usually brilliant. You're not one of those whacked-out, temperamental geniuses are you? Man, I'm having enough trouble already with the promoters and the cast. This is all I need. Man, why me?"

"Can I see the script again?" I ask.

"Here, Lady, why don't you sit down and look at it. Let me know if you come up with anything, will ya? I have to go check on the cast. They're probably back there screwing each other instead of dressing."

I like the play, and begin to sketch a set on the back of the script. Before I've completed the drawing, I look up and everything looks different.

"Hello?" I call out to the director, but he's long gone, or I'm long gone. I feel disoriented, like a basketball being palmed from left to right. I'm inside the set, the one I've just drawn. I am standing in the middle of a street. On one side is a line of newly erected buildings, all made of steel and glass. The cement of the sidewalks is newly paved white, and the lawns are all manicured in a carpet of something synthetic and gray. The people are wearing mostly crisp linens in various shades of gray,. There are sentries posted in front of each identical building; and I wonder how they know which post is theirs. Their uniforms are gray, but they hold orange rifles. The orange color looks shockingly unfriendly against this background. The people passing by don't seem to notice them, me or even each other. They all have the same little half-smile on their face, as though it was put there by the same sadistic plastic surgeon.

On the other side of the street are wooden buildings. There is a restaurant with a big orange sign declaring "THE ORANGE STREET CAFE." A General Store, a Tailor, which is boarded up with a little sign saying "Will return in September," and a pawnshop finish the street. The people are cheerfully dressed in loose-fitting garments of soft, brushed cotton, all orange. They are greeting each other and laughing. There are no sentries on this side of the street.

"That's an unusual dress you have on there, Lass." A man dressed in orange comes over to be friendly.

"Thank you." I say as I look down at what I'm wearing. It's an orange and gray checkered drop-waist. The fit is loose, but the fabric is stiff. It makes me look like a pole sporting a tent. "It's not my usual style. I..." Why do I feel I have to explain myself to this person whom I don't even know. So what if it isn't my usual style?

"Well, if you want my advice," he says, "stick with orange. You can't go wrong there."

"I'll remember that," I say, and he walks away. As if I would take fashion advice from a man dressed in head-to-toe dreamsicle. Something about this place is making me very hungry. I spot a hot dog vendor just a little way down the street and head in his direction. The dress I'm wearing has pockets, but they're empty.

"I would like a hot dog," I say to the man, "but I don't have any money."

"Oh, a pretty lass like you shouldn't go hungry. I'll give you one, on the house. My treat."

"Thank you very much," I say. "Is there any catsup or mustard?"

"Right there in front of you," he says, pointing at an orange colored sauce. "Mixed together. It's easier that way."

"Oh." I say. I eat the hot dog as though it's the first I've ever had. It's so delicious. "This is the best hot dog I've ever eaten," I tell him.

"That'll be a dollar fifty," he says.

"A dollar fifty? But I told you I don't have any money. You said it was on the house, your treat."

"Changed my mind. Don't like that dress of yours. Working both sides of the street. Now give me my dollar fifty."

"But I don't have it."

"Thief. Thief." He yells into the crowd. They start to gather around me.

"But he said I could have it," I say. They don't seem to hear me or to care. They're a mob now, with a cause. I begin to run quickly down the street. I find an alleyway. My heart is pounding fiercely. What should I do?

Before I have time to think, a door opens and a thick, muscular arm reaches out for me.

"Quickly," says a calm, reassuring voice, "in here."

"They're after me." I say, after the door shuts. "A hot dog. They think I stole a hot dog. But," I say, "he gave it to me." Panting heavily in-between words, I realize that I probably sound crazy.

"Someone gave you a hot dog and then said you stole it?" I focus on the man with the great biceps.

"Jake. Thank God it's you."

"Are you all right?" he asks. He looks concerned.

"He said he didn't like my dress." I say.

"It is kinda ugly." He grins.

"I'm so glad you grabbed me. I didn't know what to do." I still feel the pressure of his hand on my arm. Yet when I look down, it's no longer there.

"I'm glad I could help." He's standing only inches away from me. The musky smell of his cologne is filling my senses. "You know you're going to have to get rid of this." He reaches over to touch the dress. As he holds the fabric between his finger and his thumb, his finger slips under and touches my skin. He steps closer to me and leans in until we are breathing each other's breath.

Bam. Bam. Someone is pounding on the door. "Quick, under the bed," Jake says. I get under the bed as quickly as I can. My heart is still pounding from the run, and from Jake.

"We're looking for a woman in a gray and orange dress." The man's voice is booming so loudly that it echoes off the walls. "Have you seen her?"

"A gray and orange dress? That's odd. Sounds ugly," Jake says. "No. I'm sure I would remember that."

The man seems satisfied with Jake's attitude and leaves. "Be sure to shout if you see her," he says. The door slams.

"You can come out now," Jake says. "And take off that damn dress."

"Shall I walk through the streets naked?" I ask, smiling at him.

"No. That would attract almost as much attention as your dress, although not nearly as much as it would on the gray side of the street."

"They seem pretty civilized compared to what I've just experienced," I say.

"Very," he says. "I've never gone in much for the etiquette of the civilized." For a moment I get an emotionally painful deja' vous. I remember that there are social norms I find important that he doesn't.

"Here," he says. "My pants won't fit you, but see if you can do something with these two shirts." They're orange, of course. I put them on. Using the arms of one, I make a wrap-style, belted skirt. I pull the other over my head, unable to help myself from enjoying the lingering scent of Jake as the cloth caresses my nose.

Jake takes the "ugly" dress and places it in the ceiling, behind a movable tile. I hadn't noticed this hiding place before, and I wonder what else is up there.

"You lied pretty well just then," I say to him.

"Would you rather I told the truth?" he asks.

"No, of course not. You're right." I say this, but in my heart I'm sorry that it is so easy for him. I wonder what else he has lied about. I'm getting a bad ache in my stomach. I think it's the hot dog, combined with fear and suspicion. Jake's eyes look worried.

"Not here, Karina. Just hold on a minute," he says, and goes into the other room.

I replay our conversation over in my mind. I told him he was right to lie, which makes me wonder if I've always sent him this message. I wonder if, in fact, I send everyone this message. I'm not big on confrontation. Sometimes not knowing the truth is easier.

"Here, drink this." He returns with something that looks suspiciously like orange juice. The thought of drinking it is curdling my stomach, but he's giving me his insistent look.

I take a drink, close my eyes, and a tunnel appears. I step into it. Then I notice that the walls are bubbling and flowing, like lava. They look so hot, so fiercely dangerous, yet so rhythmically passionate. I watch as they churn and reabsorb themselves, reinventing their surface and recreating their world in an unending flow of self-expression. I'm mesmerized by their beauty and drawn to their dance. My excitement rises with the heat and the surge of the movement. I sense the power of creation at work and want desperately to be a part of that. The heat continues to reach toward me until the hair on my arms begins to sizzle. It hurts.

"Jake!" I call out. "Jake!"

An echo of Momma's voice comes to me saying, "beware of the walls of fire."

"Momma!" I scream.

The heat begins to subside. A cool breeze blows through the tunnel. I walk into the breeze, and find my way back into the world where Momma waits.

Momma is dabbing my arms with a gray cloth. She dips it into a bucket of water and herbs - comfrey, it smells like. Momma wraps my arms in a poultice. How did she know I would need this? I wonder. Can she really see my dreams, in advance? Momma's psychic powers have always made me feel like hiding. What scares me most is what she doesn't say. She gives a directive and then lets you figure out whether it's logical-based or otherworldly inspired. I'm growing very weary of second guessing everyone and everything.

"My arms hurt." I say.

"You went too close to the fire," Momma says. "I warned you over and over about it. You have to be careful not to let things hurt you when you're in the dream dimension. You're over-exposing yourself, Karina."

"And exactly how am I supposed to avoid that?" I ask. I'm irritated with my own lack of intuition in these matters. It's not that I lack intuition. I have it for lots of things. I just seem to lose it when Momma's involved. I suppose I could see a psychiatrist about it, but that would make Momma crazy. She doesn't think you should let people mess with your mind. We had this discussion once. I told then her that I wouldn't need someone else to mess with my mind if she would just stop jumbling it up. She didn't speak to me for a week after that. I never did see the shrink.

"Karina, you need to let go of your inhibitions. Relax into the messages while retaining your strength." Momma says.

Easy for you to say, I think.

"This journey made no sense to me whatsoever," I say. "I understood the message of the red, showing me the power of my passion. I felt the peacefulness of accepting the vulnerability of love and loss I found in pink. But this orange dream was total chaos."

"Think about the images you saw," Karina. "It's very important that you understand them. Each dream builds on the others. Sometimes that's hard to see, but you have to try. I'm here to help you, if you'd just let me. If you are going to be hard-headed and do this alone, you're going to get yourself badly hurt."

Momma knows how to hurt a person and make it seem like it's all their fault. But I know that she feels hurt when I'm hurt. Sometimes I even let myself get hurt just to hurt her. I know that this is sick behavior, and that I shouldn't do it, but it's one of the few things in life that always works.

"Take some time alone to figure out what your dream meant before tomorrow." Momma says. "I'll be in the other room, making a fresh poultice for your arms. They are not too bad, but we should keep them soothed."

I let my consciousness rest in my arms and try to comprehend how they could actually be burned in this reality when I know my physical body did not accompany me on the journey. I make a mental note: Research ethereal bodies and consciousness connections.

Mother Calloway has been on my mind a lot. I really miss her. I miss her more knowing that I can't pick up the phone and call her. She was easy to talk to. Not the kind to give advice. She just asked softly probing questions, then let you figure out the best answer. I wonder what she'd say about my orange dream. She'd pick the most obvious question: "What did you learn about yourself?"

About myself? Did I learn anything new about myself? The question lingers, but my mind keeps going back to Jake's hand on my arm, his finger on my skin. I wonder how he is doing right now, but in my heart I know that I don't have to wonder. I can feel his sadness rolling through the air like dust in the breeze.

"Karina, the poultice is ready," Momma calls, "and it's time to eat." I realize that I am famished.

"I'm coming. I'll eat anything you have." I say. "As long as it's not hot dogs."

Gramma and Auntie Connie have been cooking, as usual. They've made grilled fish and white rice. We always cook our fish outside on the grill. That way the house doesn't smell of fish the next day when we are eating chicken or beans or whatever. Gramma oils the skin of the fish so it won't stick to the foil. When I look at the oil mixing with the gray-blue of the skin, it looks like the deep waters from where the fish came. I can almost see it, swimming happily about its business, just gulping and eating and swishing through its environment. Normally, this sort of thinking would turn me off from eating it, but now I don't care. I'm too hungry to worry about whether I should eat this living thing, which in turn eats other living things to grow up to become this size for me.

"The fish will eat other fish whether or not you protest the cycle of life," Momma says. The look of exasperation she seems to reserve only for me is on her face. I know I exasperate Momma. Things are very black and white for her. She has the gift of knowing where control and chaos fit. Maybe I will ask her about this dream after all. Maybe not. It would be too much like admitting that she's right. I guess I'm not willing to admit that anyone else could be right about anything, at least not now.

The meal is delicious and Gramma is bringing out a hot blueberry pie she baked for desert. It smells heavenly. This is what a house should smell like, hot blueberry pie. I wonder why you never see that in an air freshener bottle.

Gramma serves me a slice of pie, setting a big scoop of vanilla ice cream on top without having to ask whether I want it. Of course I want vanilla ice cream. Gramma does know some things about me.

The richness of the ice cream melts with the freshness of the berries inside my mouth, and I am a contented woman.

"Have you sent a sympathy card to Jake yet?" Momma asks. She really knows how to spoil a perfect moment. I just glare at her.

"Well, it's the right thing to do; you know it is." She says.

"Thank you, Miss Manners," I say, and then regret my sarcasm. "I'm sorry, Momma. I just don't feel much like doing the right thing right now."

"You shouldn't let your feelings run your life so much, Karina," Momma says, turning away to end the conversation. It's just as well. That conversation would have gone nowhere, same as it always does. I'm tired of dealing with Momma. I'm tired of everything. I'm going to my room for the evening, to pray that I have a dreamless sleep.

June 12

Third Journal Entry: Orange

What was I doing in that color anyway? Searching for balance? Orange was chaos. Gray was control. Maybe the dream was telling me that I have to figure a way to give each of these some space inside me. According to the dream, I spend much more of my time in chaos. Big revelation! I didn't need to live through that awful dream to tell me this. There's more, though. There's always more to these dreams. Like that thing with Jake. I want both sides of everything to be black or white, but they never are. Especially I want Jake to be black or white, and especially he is not. I'm annoyed and depressed that I could smell him so distinctly, that the smell lingers with me still. And I can't believe that I came so close to tasting him again, that his touch could still melt me that way, in spite of all we've been through. How can I be attracted to a man who doesn't give me the respect or validation I need? Maybe that's part of the duality of the dream. Maybe, at some point, I have to come to terms with these conflicting emotions. Maybe.

But, what about the lava? Where did it come from? And why did I want it so badly? It felt like it was alive, like it was trying to reach me, to churn me into it and change me in some way. Of course it was. It did change me. It burned me.

Maybe that was just a psychosomatic reaction, my mind sent signals to my skin in reaction to my perceived reality. I've read about things like that happening.

The other possibility is that the two realities are not so distinct as we all want to believe. K.

Guide's Journal, Third Entry.

Karina had a close call in this color. She met the fire and didn't control it. At least she had the sense to let me come in to help her. I could feel that she was confused. Torn between running and staying. Just like she was torn between chaos and order. She's always been conflicted, always wanting to commit too heavily to either emotions or logic. I've often wondered whether this tendency has something to do with her father, Peter, and I splitting. I still love Peter. I think Karina knows that. Maybe I shouldn't have let her know it. She's never understood why we couldn't get back together, why our beliefs were a chasm, perched on edges where we weren't willing to live.

As I watch Karina now, making her way through her dreams, always tottering near the drop in the cliff, I want to run and catch her. But, I know that it's her karma she is living through. I know she has to find her own spirit and make her own choices. No one told me that being a mother would be so hard.

I think Karina saw today how polarizing one-sided thinking can be. I'm glad she's still enlisting Jake in her struggle. If they can only stay together long enough to let their images reflect that special love mirror they have, maybe they will come

to understand the lesson of this color, one of the important lessons of life. Blessed be.

I've spent the entire morning looking for an appropriate sympathy card for Jake. Nothing I read seems to work and I'm very frustrated. They are either too sweet or too spiritual or too ambiguous. I know that I should just write one myself. At least then it would say what I want it to. Except that I'm not sure I want him to hear what I really want to say. Still, I could temper it a little. I'm selling myself on this idea so that I can get the hell out of this card shop. Happily, it's working.

As I navigate my way home, a question keeps pulling at my mind: Should I drop the card quietly into the mail, or should I hand deliver it?

Chapter Four - Peach
Compassion Comes

I wonder if Jake will realize that writing this is not easy for me, that it brings back memories of all those love poems I sent to him early in our relationship, of all the letters he wrote to me. I keep them hidden in my special memory box, along with the photographs, the captured moments that I promised myself I would one day enshrine in albums and set on our coffee table for all the world to see. Of course, I never did. Now the coffee table is stored in Momma's basement, along with that box of old photos and letters. There doesn't seem to be much point in preserving anything, especially anything as transitory as pictures of points in time that have since drifted back to wherever they came from.

I'm glad in my heart to think that, unlike my pictures, Mother Calloway lives on in that place where freed souls can romp and play. The card is finished. It reads:

> "She flies on wings
> of golden peace,
> and rests in the lap of God.
>
> A shining star
> within your heart
> and mine,
> she lives on
> in the deep spaces

Rainbow Goddess: A Journey Tale

where Angels sing
and whispers whistle on the wind,

A smile
always on her lips-
the flutter of a wink
in her eye, she lives on."

I address the envelope as though I will put it in the mail. I add a stamp, still wondering if it will be necessary.

"I'm taking a walk," I tell Momma. "I won't be long."

I walk around the block, tempting myself to stick the card in the corner mailbox. "If I haven't mailed it by the time I get home," I tell myself, "I'll get in the car and drive it over to Jake's."

Losing myself in the rhythm of my pace, I let my body follow its fear and drop the card in the big blue box.

I arrive at home, reluctant to go in, and look down at my hands. Empty.

Momma is waiting for me when I enter.

"There you are, Karina," Momma says, "It's time to take your journey."

To me, this sounds like: "It's time to take your medicine." I really need to get a better attitude about this journey if I am going to continue with it. The journey through orange left a taste in my mouth that is still hard to swallow. I haven't prepared myself for the peach trip at all. I'm supposed to meditate, to settle my mind and open up my thoughts before each journey. Momma says that I will have better control of my lessons if I meditate. I may be cynical, but I resist the idea that I have an influence over what happens while I'm "gone dreamin'," as Gramma calls it. Somehow, I'm more comfortable believing that things just happen in the color world.

I'm locking the bathroom door. Tonight I've decided to take my time and enjoy my bath. After all, this is my journey and not Momma's. I'm locking the door. It gives me perverse pleasure to think of her standing there outside the door, holding the black, embroidered robe--waiting.

I want to shake this thought because I'm beginning to think I've inherited her temperament, something I've spent my whole life despising. You spend years fighting your Mother, then one day you wake up and you are her. I've noticed this in my girlfriends too. It's a trick of nature. Well, it won't happen to me. Momma is a rigid and closed woman, so I am going to be deliberately loose and open.

Taking deep breaths, I feel the rose perfume roaming through my body like a welcome houseguest. I use my relaxation technique of counting to ten, letting go of sections of my body with each number, starting with my eyes.

Momma must have sensed my irritation because she is being gentler with me than usual. She takes a moment to rub my neck a little after placing the robe on my back. Then, she takes me by the hand, leading me to the mat. The Goddess is waiting as always: Austere and beautiful. She is the kind of woman you can't quite get a handle on. The kind of woman I want to be, but fear her strength too much to become.

"Karina, before you begin," Momma says, "I need to tell you something." She looks very serious.

"Remember when I told you to be careful not to touch the walls of the tunnel?"

"Yeah, I remember that."

"Yes, well, even though you didn't touch the walls in orange, you got too close to the walls and they touched you."

"You mean they seemed to touch me."

"They did touch you, Karina. The tunnel is the connection between the two worlds. At some point, you are going to have to master it. I was hoping we wouldn't have to deal with this quite so soon. You have such a lot to learn. Really, I'm afraid you're not as ready as I'd hoped. You're still resisting."

"Master it how?"

"That depends," she says. "Every tunnel is different, just like every person is different. What is the same is that it's the tool of your purification. In it and through it you find your strengths and weaknesses. When you learn to mold these together, your spirit will become like gold, positives and negatives aligned, perfect in itself, impervious to misalignment."

"Wait. In the tunnel I turn to gold?"

"Well, metaphorically, yes. The tunnel is the tool of your purification. I don't know how to explain this to you until you've learned more in your dreams. For now, just try to go as quickly through the tunnel as possible, without touching it. And try to think good thoughts while you're in there."

"Momma, maybe I really shouldn't be doing this. If it's so dangerous, why would you want me to risk it?"

"Karina, I promise you that, if you keep on this journey, what you learn will change the way you look at life. Many of the worries you have now will fall right out of your life. You will come to see that they are completely unimportant. It will be worth the risk."

She seems to believe what she says. And I really want to believe her. I just wish she didn't make it sound so scary.

"All right. I'll keep going."

Momma starts chanting. Holding the Crystal Goddess in my hands, I recite my rhyme to the color peach.

"Guardian of humanity
protect the ungloved,
Bringing a cloak
of peace from above.

Carry compassion
on wings from afar,
Beheld from the Lady
who sits on a star.

Sharer of Charity
Champion true
Shower your gentleness,
raining me new..."

I am in a place where the sun shines peach and the trees are filled with baskets, the fruit already picked and laid in them. The air is heavy with the sweet and sour of the first ripe bite of fruit.

"Hello," says a voice. "I'm glad you could join me. I've made a brandy of the bruised ones. It's been fermenting a year now."

The man is short and round and very happy with himself and his product. I can see that I will not get away without taking a taste.

He offers me the bottle, which he has already drunk from. It is an old Chianti jug. The bottom is wrapped in wide pieces of straw. Wrapped as it is, the bottle seems not so fragile and more willing to be handled than a standard wine jug. He lifts the jug to his lips one more time, as if to show me how to drink, but before he takes his long swig, he says, "To your journey, Darling."

His face does not twist and grimace, but his tongue seems to be dancing inside his mouth.

The jug now offered, I take a sip. It has more kick than I expected, and making a face, I say, "To my journey."

I am on an island, in ancient ruins. Lining the walls are beautifully crafted clay pots in every size and shape imaginable. They are all a peachy color. The stone-carved walls are painted with pictures of richly dressed women, arms and shoulders connected to each other, as if they are in a long, train-like parade.

I am in the center of what looks to be a courtyard or some type of community gathering place. There are stone benches and plants scattered everywhere. The flowering plants all have peach blossoms. People are slowly meandering in and out in long, flowing peach clothing. There are stairs leading up to another level at each of the entrances. Everyone seems happy and peaceful. I feel out of place. These people belong to a different time than I am used to. They seem to be very aware of each other, almost connected like the women on the walls.

Suddenly, everyone is turning toward one of the entrances. A man has appeared wearing heavy armor. I recognize his form as that of the Greek god, Zeus. I recognize his face too. His eyes are blue and his hair is black. His mouth is set in a severe frown. I am familiar with his unhappiness. He has the face of Jake.

"Give me your attention," he is saying. "I have a proclamation. You have all been misled. Your sole honoring of the Earth Goddess has offended the Gods and we will no longer tolerate your neglect. The Earth Goddess is not your mother. She is not the creator of fertility you have worshipped her as. Behold. I show you Athena, who springs from me whole. I, a male, am your rightful God. From now and forever you will honor me."

Watching this spectacle closely, I can see that Zeus is using light and shadow to create his illusion. But the others do not seem to notice this. They are afraid of his arrogance and threats. They seem so vulnerable in comparison to him. I want to stand up and expose him, but I don't know what he will do to this sensitive, docile community if I do. He is awfully angry about his position.

Groups of armor-bearing men have now gathered at each of the other entrances, and I can see that there are more behind them.

"History begins today," Zeus is saying. "Let it write that men are the rulers of this Earth."

Army or no army, this is too galling for me to take. This is how it begins and I have seen the end. Mother Earth gets raped, almost beyond our ability to ever heal her.

"You're a fraud." I call out. "Anyone can see this is a trick. You are lying. You may have power, but life does not grow in your belly."

"You are brave, Misguided One. Come here," Zeus says to me. His eyes follow each step I take.

Now I've done it. Nearing him, I stop when I get about ten feet away. He hasn't taken his eyes off me yet.

"Come closer." He says. I let my eyes meet his. I can see the wheels of his brain whirling up waves behind the blue of those pools. What will he do? I wonder.

When I get close enough, he reaches out, grabs me and begins to whisper in my ear. "I like you, blond one, you look regal and you have spunk, so I will give you a choice. You can come with me and be my wife, or I will kill you now."

Some choice. If I died now, what would be the point? I have obviously had no impact on this crowd with my allegations. They look as bewildered as ever. Still, if Zeus kills me, maybe something will spark and I will have changed the course of history. I look into the eyes of the group. Definitely a long shot.

If I go with Zeus, I may be able to persuade him to be gentler with the Earth. It's all I can do.

"I'll go with you," I tell him.

I don't want to admit it, but I am strangely attracted to his maleness. I almost feel sorry for his feelings of jealously and abandonment. Also, I'm having trouble resisting that face.

We ride off on his white horse, accompanied by his army. When we reach his home, I'm surprised to see that it is a well-kept castle. My rooms are ornately decorated, bronzed and gilded with miles of rich, velvet drapes. If I hadn't been manipulated into being here, I might actually be comfortable.

I feel strangely suspended in Zeus' world. It's as though I float on a string of moments, like notes across a sheet of music. I am not the music, but I am on the edge of it. Like looking at life through a window, I can see it but not smell it. I feel a stir in my belly when I'm with Zeus. I keep thinking it will mount itself into something more, but I'm numb to further sensations. I feel I'm forever in that place between sleep and waking. I want desperately to wake up, but just don't have the energy. It is as though some great curtain is blocking my view of reality, but I just can't pull the cord to open it. What am I afraid of? What does Zeus have to do with this fear? Is he the cause of the fear, or just an able mirror reflecting it back to me?

The sun is settling into the horizon. It looks so contented, knowing where it is going, easy in its rhythms of day and night.

"Karina, my wife, how was your day?" Zeus asks.

"It was nice. I spent it in the garden, writing poetry. The peach blossoms are all in bloom, and the air smells really sweet. How was your day, Zeus, my husband?"

Zeus likes to be called "my husband." It makes him feel like he's in charge, or maybe just that I'm really his wife; I'm never certain. For a god of his strength and power, he is pretty unsure of himself. He puts on a great front, though. Most people don't seem to notice his vulnerability, but I see it.

"I had to subdue an uprising in Athens. It was a long day. I am glad to be home - with you."

Zeus really seems to love me, and I really care for him, misguided as he is. We have some kind of a soul connection.

"I wrote a little verse about you. Would you like to hear it?"

"It is about me? Yes."

This verse is really of the greeting card variety, which I so disdain, but Zeus is not into real poetry.

"Thy arms are strong
but gentle and kind.
Cunning, yet loving
is thy mind.
Thy soul has a depth
no one can find.
Thou art a challenge
great Zeus of mine."

I know that Zeus likes to think of himself as a challenge, and that this piece will feed his ego. That is, after all, the whole point: to keep his frustration level down to where he will do the least damage.

Zeus is pleased with my gift. He holds my face in his hands and looks deeply into my eyes. When he touches me this way, I forget that he can sometimes be a child, demanding to be the center of the universe. I forget that he uses crude and cruel methods to reach his goals. I even forget that there are many little things about him that annoy me. At this moment I remember only that his eyes are the bluest I have ever seen, and that I am perfectly happy to be lost inside them. I follow their path, the path that winds round and round my heart. The blue of his eyes is fading to peach, and the swirling path has become a cobblestone road with a stone hedge along it. As I walk, the hedge gradually builds itself into a wall, and then into a tunnel. I am nearly to the light by the time its self-construction is complete. I feel very peaceful as I walk through the light. When I look up, I see Momma's face.

Momma is still being sweet, and it's beginning to dawn on me that my moods through the journey affect her moods, as if she is taking this journey along with me. I don't think that she can get into my mind, although I suppose that's possible. I do know she is somehow linked in with my emotions.

"Are you all right, Karina?"

"Yes, Momma. I'm fine."

"That journey was long," Momma says.

I'm beginning to focus again. I look around and notice that the candles are nearly out. I can see a bright moon and stars through the window.

"It didn't seem long. Truthfully, I'm almost sorry to be back. It's not that I would leave you, Momma. It's just that I actually had a life and a purpose in that dream."

"You have a life and a purpose here too, Karina. You are supposed to be using the dreams to uncover it."

"I thought I was just supposed to find myself." I say.

"Uncovering your purpose in life is part of finding yourself. But not all of it." Momma adds.

"Why does everything have to be so complicated?" I ask.

"Taken together, life can be complicated, but each piece is simple. Think about your dreams and you will learn to understand this. Anyway, enough talk for now." Momma is back to her abrupt self. "It's time for you to eat something. Gramma and Auntie Connie have gone to sleep, but we can re-heat the dinner they left."

The dinner is chicken cooked in a leeks and brandy sauce, served with wild rice and asparagus tips. There is some sautéed eggplant set off to the side as a garnish. Gramma has arranged the plates and wrapped them in plastic. All we have to do is warm them in the microwave. Momma and I know we are very lucky to have Gramma.

I tell Momma that I'm going to watch some television before bed. She seems relieved, as though she's in the armed service and someone has dismissed her early from duty.

✤ ✤ ✤

June 13

Fourth Journal Entry, Peach

My memory is struck by the contrast between the men and women in the ancient time I visited. The influence of matriarchal society was still so strong that even the fighting was more civilized than it is today. Or maybe it was just the setting that made it seem so. I feel silly to admit this, but I miss Zeus. I know he was wrong in his need to control, but he really needed me. And that was kind of nice.

Learn. Learn. What did I learn? I guess I learned that it's easier to have compassion for people than I thought. I really cared about everyone, including Zeus. I found myself not quite as willing to judge as I usually am. Having that compassion kind of colored my world.

I am again left with more questions than answers: Could it have been my compassion that made the whole world seem gentler? Do my emotions, does my intent, change the tone and texture of the world I am in? And does that happen only in dream states, or does it happen in "the real world" as well? Is there even a difference between the reality of the dream world and the world I think of as the real one?

If we truly impact our worlds to the extent that we help create them, I have a lot of changing to do. I have no way of knowing whether my being in Zeus' world really made an impact on it, but for the first time in my life, I'd like to think it did. K.

June 13

Guides Journal, Fourth Entry

Karina came back when the candles were low. She didn't seem to notice the passage of time. I followed her as best I could, but she fell in love with Zeus and didn't notice anything outside of that. I know she felt she was doing it for the right reason. Karina always has a reason for the things she does. That it often makes sense only to her doesn't seem to bother her. In any event, she was the soul of kindness. I hope that she saw that when she is not hiding behind her fears, she is a truly sweet and caring person. I think Karina does not give herself enough credit for her attributes.

I will have to remember to stress again the importance of her watching the time she spends in a color. I don't want her to end up like cousin Cura, leaving her body forever for a transitional world. Blessed be.

The telephone rings.

"Karina, it's for you."

"Hello."

"Hi, Karina."

"Jake. I - umm - how are you?"

"I'm okay. I called to thank you for the card. It was really nice. And to thank you for being so nice about the burial plot."

Is he saying "nice" as though he's surprised that I could actually be such a thing, or am I imagining it?

"You're welcome," I say. "I couldn't find a card that I wanted to buy."

"I know," Jake says. "They're all so lame." Did he actually say that? I'm astounded that he even noticed.

"Yeah," I say. "Jake, you sound different,"

"How?"

"I don't know. You sound sort of softer, more sensitive." Oh, God. I hope that didn't come out wrong. He's laughing.

"What's so funny?" I ask.

"Oh, I don't know. Just the way you said 'sensitive,' like I was from a planet where sensitive couldn't exist."

"I'm sorry," I say. "I didn't mean it like that."

"Karina, Karina? There must be something wrong with my phone. I thought I just heard you say you were sorry," he says. Now it's my turn to laugh.

"Sounds strange, doesn't it?" I say.

"Yeah, but it's nice." There's that word again, nice.

"This is the most civilized conversation we've had in months." I say. "Why do you think that is?"

"I guess neither of us has much left to prove," he says.

"Funny how that happens." As I say this, I get a picture of Zeus in my mind. I see the blue of his eyes, Jake's eyes, and I remember how looking in them made all his rough edges seem unimportant.

"Karina, I know we've really hurt each other, and neither of us wants to re-live that, but - I don't know what I really want to say. I guess I just don't want it to be like we don't know each other."

"I don't want it to be like that, either. What do you suggest, Jake?"

"I'd really like it if we could still be friends."

It hurts to hear this. Even though it's an olive branch of sorts, I just can't help feeling the emptiness from the missing part of the relationship. Like a phantom limb, the ache and itch of it haunt me.

"I'd like to be friends too," I say. "But to be honest, I'm not sure I'm up to that right now."

"Karina, I know we have different ways of looking at things; I just think maybe we can both learn something about our mistakes by getting to know each other again. You seem like such a stranger to me and I don't like that. How about we just give it a try?"

There is silence while I try to figure out where this is going.

"We could meet for lunch tomorrow," he says. My treat. I know you're out of work and all. Just lunch, and I promise to be good. Please?"

'Please?' Did I really hear 'please?' I'm asking for trouble, but I really do like this man. And he did just lose his mother.

"Well, you know I don't want to be enemies, and this town is a little small for us to pretend that we're strangers, so I guess we should try for friends. Where do you want to meet?"

"How about Vango's?"

"Okay. Vango's. Can we make it twelve o'clock? I know they're busy then, but I have to be back for something."

"Twelve's okay with me. See you then."

I hang up the phone and suddenly there is a boulder in my throat, and I find my face is raining little pebble tears. It's been a few weeks since the divorce was final and I haven't really allowed myself a good cry over it. I cried plenty when I made the decision to divorce Jake, and even more before I made it. Now, I'm wondering if I did the right thing. With a little more effort, could we have made it work? No, this anti-climax would not have come without the climax. We are both good people, but we had become toxic for each other: jealous, suspicious, defensive of every word, even cruel. I'm glad that phase of our relationship is over. And I'm not going to get myself in that position again. Still, what he said and the tenderness in his voice touched something in me, and it won't seem to let go. The last thing I think before I cry myself to sleep is that it's awful how people can get such a hold on you.

Chapter Five - Yellow
Making Mind

It's twelve o'clock noon, and I'm sitting in Vango's, waiting. I knew Jake would be late, but I came on time anyway, just in case. It's just as well; gives me a moment to collect myself.

Jake is coming toward the table. His jeans fit him nicely, but I can't help imagining him in the garb of Zeus. It's astonishing how interchangeable my worlds are becoming.

"Sorry I'm late," Jake says.

"It's all right," I say.

"Really? You're not upset?"

"No. Are you disappointed?"

"Hardly," he says, laughing. "How's everything?"

"Everything's okay. How you doing?"

"Still adjusting."

We look at each other in silence for a while, neither of us sure of what to say. "Well, I knew this would be awkward," Jake says.

"How are your sisters?" I ask.

"They're okay. Kind of clingy, though. They spend every minute together since Mom died."

"Well, at least their family loyalty is intact. Neither of them has spoken to me since we broke up. I'm sure they blame me for everything." I give him a half smile. "Of course, they've never seen you as anything other than perfect."

"That's not true, Karina."

"What, that the divorce is my fault, or that you're not perfect?"

"Please, let's not start," Jake says.

"You're right," I say. "I'm sorry."

The waitress comes back and Jake orders a cudighi. I get pizza. We smile at each other because this is the same thing we always order when we eat here.

There is more silence while I consider what topic is fair game for conversation.

"You know, the strangest thing happened to me this morning," I say. "I was jogging through the park near my house and, as I passed by this jogger, I saw a flash of your sister, Anne, in my head. It was eerie how clear it was. I wanted to stop him and ask him if he knew her."

"Were you alone?" Jake asks.

"Yeah. Well, except for him."

"Why were you jogging alone in the park? You know there was a mugging in that park just last week," he says.

"Jake, I'm trying to share a moment here, and you go into protector mode. I'm a big girl. If we're going to be friends, I need to be able to tell you about a jog in the park without you going all macho on me. This is exactly why we broke up in the first place. You're always trying to control me."

"I'm not trying to control you. I just don't want to see you get hurt," he says. "Anyway, I thought we broke up because you didn't like my job."

"It wasn't just your job," I say. I want to tell him that no one could possibly hurt me as much as he has, but I'm trying to play nice. The truth is, we hurt each other, although I have trouble remembering this.

"I didn't mean to jump on you," I say. "I'm just a little edgy lately."

"Why?"

I look at him for a long moment, trying to decide whether to tell him. "I don't know. I can't really say."

"You can tell me," he says, looking straight into my eyes with those baby blues. He always did know when I needed to talk.

"Well," I say, "Remember how Momma was always hounding me about the family journey?"

"Yeah, I remember," he says, making a snorting sound with his nose.

"Well, I'm doing it."

"Karina," he says, his voice rising so that the other diners turn to look at us. His brows close together in that way that I don't like. "Have you lost your mind? You know that shit is dangerous. It's like - like doing drugs or something."

"It's not that bad." I say, although the analogy is pretty accurate.

"If it's not that bad, then why are you so edgy?"

"I'm just having a little trouble understanding the dreams."

"Isn't your mother supposed to help you with that?"

"Yeah," I say, "but I can't really talk to her. You know that."

"So, what you're telling me is, you have decided to go on this strange mind-trip with the voodoo doll all by yourself?"

"Well, Momma's there. I just have trouble discussing it with her."

"But isn't that supposed to be the point? Aren't you going inside your head to try to figure out what's in there? Dissect it, as if that were actually possible?" He lowers his head and shakes it at the table. "Honestly, Karina, I don't know what goes on inside your brain. If it was possible to see it, I wouldn't mind having a ticket to that show."

Should I tell him that he's had tickets all along, ringside? No.

"There's more to the journey than I thought," I say.

"Well, can you stop?"

"No. I mean I could if I wanted to, but I don't want to. I'm sort of intrigued by the dreams. When I'm in there it's so real. I'm actually getting to where they're becoming lucid."

"You mean they haven't been?" His tone is rising now. I'm beginning to feel like the opening act at a dinner theater, and it makes me very uncomfortable. "You were messing around in your mind and you didn't even know you were dreaming? Even Carlos Castanada knew when he was on a peyote trip."

"I should've known better than to tell you. You take such a negative approach to everything," I say.

"I do not. I just don't happen to think screwing with your brain is the smartest thing to do."

"Oh, so now I'm dumb?"

"No. If I thought you were dumb, I would have expected something like this from you, Karina."

"Forget it. Just forget it. I shouldn't have told you in the first place."

"Karina, I just think you should stop is all."

"Oh, is that all? Is that fucking all? Well, no! I won't! Stop trying to control me, Jake." Getting up to leave, I slam my napkin on the table.

I'm almost to the door when I think about saying: "You can't tell me what to do anymore. In case you haven't noticed, we're not married." But, I stop myself. I've already had a little too much "public" in my private life for one day. It's enough that I got up and left before he could influence me, yet again, to do something I didn't want to. I hate the way people try to manipulate me.

My private phone is ringing again. I haven't answered it in weeks and I know that I should.

I watch it, willing it to stop. Why don't I want to answer it? Why does a piece of machinery that once felt like a friend now feels like an intruder, invading my space? The truth is that I don't want to share my space with anyone right now, friend or foe.

Whoever it is, they know I'm here. They're not hanging up.

The ringing won't stop. Damn it! Maybe it's important. Maybe it's Jake.

"Hello," I say.

"Karina? Are you all right? I thought maybe you fell off the face of the Earth."

"Hi, Joan. Yeah, I'm fine. How you doin'?"

"Good. I called to see if you want to go to hear Jim and Ray play tonight?"

"Thanks, Joan, but I really don't think so."

"You know, Karina, you can't stay holed up at your Momma's for the rest of your life. So you got a divorce. It happens to the best of us. It would do you good to get out."

"I'm just not ready. You remember how it felt."

"Yeah, I also remember that it didn't do me any good to hide," Joan says.

"Good or bad, I really don't want to see anyone," I say.

"All right. Have it your way."

"Thanks for calling anyway, Joan. It's good to hear your voice."

"Call me sometime, Karina."

"I will. Bye."

"Bye."

I look at the phone, back on its receiver. What is it about divorce that makes isolation feel so compelling?

I've been sitting here watching the Goddess statue for the last half-hour, trying to figure out where she gets all her power. When the afternoon sun hits her, the light splits apart into a beautiful rainbow. Each color is clear and intense. I feel drawn in a special way to the ones I've journeyed through.

I feel badly about how things went with Jake this afternoon. I don't know what got into me. I knew better than to tell him about the journey. But, just for a moment, he seemed so open; and as usual my emotions took over.

The black robe is laid out on the bed and I can hear Momma drawing my bath, so I know it's almost time to journey again.

The familiar rose scent is filling the room. I know I will soon be in another place. I hope that this will be a kinder, gentler place. I'm not good at this emotional stuff.

"Karina, it's time." Momma says. She is looking at me in a strange, appraising way. "Are you okay?" she asks. "Is there anything you want to ask me?"

"No. I'm fine," I say.

We both take our places on the mats. Momma begins chanting. I hold the Goddess and recite my rhyme to the color yellow.

"Searcher of heavens
for voices
to sing;
Scanner of cosmos
intelligence
bring;
Star gazer, brightly
enlighten
my mind,
Shine me
together
forever
in time.

I am standing in a field of tall, yellow wheat. Above me the sun is as big as the sky. Tiger swallowtail butterflies flit around me, all yellow and black. I look for a person and listen for a voice, but I am alone. The only sound is the babble of a nearby brook. I follow the sound to the edge of a gently sloping hill. Beside the brook, I see a large tray with a single glass and a lone napkin on it. When I get to it, I see that the glass is filled with yellow lemonade, and the napkin has writing on it. It reads, "Have a nice journey." I am parched from the heat of this huge sun. I toast myself and drink the lemonade.

I'm in a church. The stained glass windows are all made of yellow, and the altar is surrounded by arrangements of daffodils and dandelions. It's strange to see them together, spring babies and summer weeds. I have forgotten what I came to pray about. The church bells are ringing and a priest is entering. His vestments are yellow, and he is clearly intending to give Mass. I look around. I am the only one here.

"Let us pray," he begins. He is saying the Mass to me alone. I can't believe this. It's been a while since I've been to church and I hope that I remember all the right responses. What will he do if I don't respond, or if I respond incorrectly? I look for a prayer book, but there are none. I suppose I could leave, but that seems pretty rude, and maybe even sacrilegious. I remember the stories of God's punishment I heard as a little girl and decide to stay.

"Let us recite together the Apostle's Creed." He is saying.

"I believe in one God, the Father, the Almighty, the maker of Heaven and Earth..."

I am really glad that I remember this, and a little ashamed that I'm not sure that I believe it at all, or at least not all of it.

"...Of all that is seen and unseen." The seen part I don't mind, it's the unseen that worries me.

"...On the third day he rose again, in fulfillment of the scriptures..." This, I have never doubted. Jesus is my hero. Just as you cannot tell a child that superman cannot fly or see through buildings, I could never believe that Jesus did not rise again.

"He will come again in glory to judge the living and the dead and his kingdom will have no end..." This judgment thing has always bothered me. I mean, on the most basic level I believe it. Every action causes a reaction. What you put out is what you get back, and all of that. I'm just not sure that God waits until the end. This is exactly why I don't come to church too often. I think too much when I am here. I should look for a way out. I haven't brought a purse and I'll have nothing to give for the offering. Anyway, who will collect it?

Thankfully, he has skipped the offertory and is now blessing the Body and Blood of Christ. I watch as his hands lift the sacraments toward the heavens, and wonder why he doesn't think that God is in the Earth. Momma thinks that the Goddess is in the Earth. I think they are both everywhere, but no one has ever asked me.

The priest's eyes jerk from their tender resting on the Blood of Christ to the center isle of the church. Someone is entering. It's a man in a long, yellow robe. His hair is brown and flowing. At first I think it's Jesus, but he doesn't feel the way I imagined the presence of Jesus would feel. He stops when he is beside me and says, "Do not be afraid," which makes me think that he is an angel. They always say that, "Do not be afraid." His face looks very familiar, but in a surreal kind of way. He looks like an old picture I've seen of Jake in his high schooldays, except older. Jake was a hippie in high school. I've always admired him for that.

The Jake-angel reaches toward me and cups my head in his hands and lifts my head from my body. Just takes it right off my neck and sets it - me, well, the top of me - onto the pew. The bottom of me is still standing there.

"What in the hell are you doing?" I demand, blasphemy in church and all. I can't help it. For God's sake, he's just completely separated me. I can't help but think of the irony of his pulling me apart and his resemblance to a younger Jake.

"You think too much with your brain," he says. "This will teach you to be more whole."

"More whole? You just cut me into parts. Well, not exactly cut, but you just separated me. How did you do that, anyway?" I, my head I,-am asking, sitting all alone on the pew, still trying to analyze every action in my universe.

"It is only atoms," he responds. Some stayed to form your head, the rest are forming your body."

My body. That's right. It is still my body. I am the head and I can still control it. "Hands," I say, "put me back on my neck."

My body turns toward me now, a very scary sight. My right hand points its index finger out and moves it from side to side. It is saying "no." My body is disobeying, no, deserting me. How can that be? I watch as my feet, my legs, my torso, my arms move out into the aisle. My feet are dancing and my arms are flapping as though they are going to take off and fly. Are they all so glad to be rid of me? I am thinking this, but at the same time I know the answer, because I can sense the joy the rest of my body is experiencing, even though it's not attached.

Boy, my head sure is a downer. Or is it? Actually, my eyes and my ears and my nose and my mouth would rather be over there with the rest of my body. But, the angel told them to stay here, with my brain.

I am beginning to realize that I don't think of my body as the real me. I think of it more like a subjugate me, and it's clearly very unhappy with the arrangement.

The angel is holding the "head" me now, so that I can watch my body, which is doing cartwheels down the aisle. The priest, I notice, is frozen in place. He is watching this entire spectacle, clearly amazed at what he sees.

I am amazed too. This is the same body that didn't have enough energy to fold the laundry yesterday and "fluffed" it three times before finally deciding to leave it for Gramma. This is the body I pump full of vitamins late at night, while Momma looks on disapprovingly, in hopes that they will motivate it to get up earlier in the morning. Dancing and doing cartwheels because it doesn't have "me," the head, to weigh it down.

"Am I that bad?" I ask the angel.

"Worse," he assures me, with a smile on his face.

"Thanks." I say. "But how is my body functioning without me? Doesn't it need intelligence?" I ask.

"Surely you don't still think that the atoms of your brain are the only atoms capable of intelligence?" He asks.

Like a flash of yellow light, the proverbial bulb shines and I see what he is saying.

"Well, on an absolute level, I suppose they are basically the same."

"Now you've got it." He smiles and carries me up to where the priest is frozen in place. He takes the broken bread and offers it to me saying, "the Body of Christ."

"Amen," I say, and offer my tongue to receive it.

My body has come back now to join the "head" me. As the angel places us together, I am thankful and humble and energized.

The angel fades from solid form to a white-yellow light. The light passes into a hole in the air, forming a vortex. I follow it into the vortex and watch as the tunnel walls swirl around themselves. The walls emanate light. I want to know what makes them glow. I put my hand out, and then I remember hearing Momma's voice. "Go as quickly as you can; and don't touch the walls," she said.

I put my hand down and move toward the opening at the end of the tunnel.

Momma is eyeing me with a queer look on her face. I am aware of every inch of my person, and it feels good.

"You seem more connected," she says.

"Yeah, I feel more connected," I say. I feel connected, but there is a part of me that will need to be reminded that it's okay to share the load. I know that my brain often feels overworked and overwhelmed, but it still isn't happy about not being the center of the universe. I guess I'll have to work on that.

"How was the tunnel?" Momma asks.

"It was beautiful. Made of light."

Momma smiles. "Gramma and Auntie Connie are in the yard watching the sky. It's very clear tonight. The Goddess' light show. Why don't you join them? I'll be out in a few minutes."

Gramma, Auntie Connie and Momma know all about the stars and the moon. They know the phases and how the planets align at different times of the year. Sometimes I think they know things about the sky that even the stars don't know. I like to sit and listen to their stories. I sit on the glider and let them lull me into ancient times.

June 14

Fifth Journal Entry: Yellow

I find my hand reaching frequently for my neck, making sure that it's still attached. I can't help but wonder at the irony of Jake being the one to show me how to become whole again by taking me apart. In secret, I hope that maybe that is what's happening in my "real" life. That Jake's pushing me over the edge of leaving him - which has given me the space in which to take this journey-might somehow bring a happy ending. Of course, I stopped believing in fairy tales a long time ago. But that doesn't mean I can't still hope for them.

I'm very intrigued about how my body and my mind interact. I understand the physics of it. I just have a little challenge getting my mind around the metaphysics. If the various parts of me can separate and leave, that means that the entire world is not solid. While I know this is technically true, I still like to think of my reality as solid. Which leads to the question: Is my reality true? Are there people running around the planet slipping through doors and rocks, or, even stranger, mentally willing atoms together? Am I some kind of lower metaphysical life form?

I guess the more important lesson of the journey wasn't what other people do. It's: What do I do? I can't believe how disconnected I've been and how draining that was. When I let my body and my mind work together, it's a very freeing existence. I'm going to try to hold this thought. K.

June 14

Guide's Journal, Fifth Entry

Karina had her first taste of body liberation today. I thought she took it rather well. I must confess, I was a little taken aback at the lesson myself. I've seen many people leave their bodies, but never a body leaving them. Karina, of course, is always different.

It was interesting that she chose Jake to perform the separation. She must still trust him much more than she lets on. Or, maybe she's only seeing the physical action of it, feeling as though he's cut her in some way. This would be a natural reaction too. Still, her subconscious would never have let him do it if she didn't trust him deep down.

She reconnected well, and seems more comfortable with her energies flowing as they are. I'm praying she will maintain this level of physical awareness. She came through the light tunnel untouched. Thank the Goddess for that. Blessed be.

Chapter Six - Sea Green
Releasing Reason

One selling point for this journey is that my skin has become softer and younger looking from the daily rose oil baths. My relaxation techniques seem to come more easily in this setting. Too bad that I can't spend all my time here.

"Karina," Momma says, in her beckoning tone.

"Yes, Momma," I say.

Duty calls.

The room has new candles, as usual, the color of my journey. Tonight they are a light, sea green. They look like pillars of seawater.

"Have I ever told you about the Tao?" Momma asks.

"The Tao? You mean as in Taoism?"

"Yes," she says.

"Isn't that an eastern religion?" I ask.

"It's an eastern religion, but a universal principle. The idea is that there is a way, a flow, an ordering principle in all of life. Life has a rhythm. We live within that rhythm. If you flow with it, you will be safe within the Tao."

"I get the idea," I say.

"Good. Do you think you can remember it when you travel through this tunnel?"

"I'll try."

Momma squints her eyes and looks at me hard, as if her concentration can be transferred into me.

"Let's begin," she says softly.

I pick up the Goddess statue. She is cool to my touch. She begins to warm as I recite my rhyme to sea green.

> *"Caller to modesty,*
> *Seeker of truth;*
> *Teacher, Philosopher,*
> *Waker of youth,*
> *Wrap me inside of*
> *your benevolent light.*
> *Brighten my vision,*
> *as day becomes night."*

I'm sitting at a sidewalk cafe. The waiter is coming toward me with a smile on his face. He sets a parfait glass in front of me and explains that it's from the gentleman a few tables over. The drink is a "grasshopper." Creme de menthe and ice cream. I look at my giftor and he is having one too. He raises his glass and mouths the words, "To your journey."

I watch as his lips wrap themselves around the glass. His eyes are closed as though the rich chill of this drink is a special sensation. I copy his actions and realize that he's right.

I am in an ocean of gorgeous, clear, sea green liquid. I'm swimming near a coral reef and can see schools of parrotfish and mahi-mahi sharing my water. I've been under the surface for some time now, and am surprised that I can hold my breath this long. As I swing my body around to follow a sound in the water, I become aware that something is different, wrong. Something is wrong. My legs are not legs. They are covered with scales. My feet are fins. What? I'm a mermaid? I don't remember being a mermaid.

The sound that I heard is coming closer now. It sounds like a motor. I guess that would mean it's a boat, since I'm a long way from shore. I swim closer to the surface to get a look at my company. It's an old fishing boat. She's heading away from me and her name is Esmerelda. I see only one man aboard. He's wearing a captain's hat and standing at the helm. He turns to look behind, then spots me watching him. He's starting the long circle now that will bring his boat around. Do I know him? As he gets closer I can see that he is an older man, maybe sixty. His face is weathered in that cracked-leather way that people get who work outside their whole lives. He is close enough that I can see his every move. The Esmerelda is an old fishing boat. He cuts the motor and is working with the nets. If he's going to fish here he won't have much luck. The schools of fish all heard his motor and swam away. If he would ask me, I would tell him this. Maybe he didn't see me after all. I go under to see what his net looks like and realize that it is made for very large fish. I guess he didn't want the mahi-mahi and the parrot after all. But there are no other fish here.

Suddenly I realize that I am, technically, a fish. He did see me. The captain has restarted his motor and the large net is headed in my direction. I have no idea how fast I can swim, but I flap my tail for all it's worth. I'm in the center of this large curtain of rope and am swimming at a diagonal, away from the oncoming danger of that looming trap. I swim toward the edge of the net. I am a pretty fast swimmer, but that boat is many times my match. I'm almost to the edge of the rope, but the boat is over me now. The net is dragging just slightly back from it. In another couple of seconds I will be caught.

No, it's past.

I'm free.

I feel the rough brush of rope against the ends of my fin as I swish my way toward safer waters.

There is an island nearby, and some of the older mountains are under the water. I'm close to a rock that has an indentation. It's not quite a cavern but will have to do for now. When I think the coast is clear, I risk rising to the surface to see what happened to my predator. The Esmerelda is still there, sitting like a cat waiting to be fed. She is a ways away, but my vision is pretty good. I can't see any movement on the deck. Maybe the captain has abandoned his hunt.

I hear strange, high-pitched clicking noises, and turn to follow their direction. I see, off at a distance, a line of other mermaids. They are shaking their heads and clicking at me, as though I have broken some sacred code of the mermaid clan.

Before I have a chance to ask what I've done, I turn and I see. Beside me a man in a black scuba suit has a syringe with a large needle in it, poised for injection. I twist to move away, but he catches me in the soft of my side with that icy steel point. His arms surround me, then I feel my body go limp.

I have a hammering headache. Looking around, I see a machine in the corner pumping bubbles into my water. I swim over to the water's edge and touch behind it to feel what I already knew would be glass. I'm in an aquarium. Trapped. At least they had the decency to color the water the pleasant sea green of my ocean home. Whoever arranged this must have studied my environment, my habits, the way a laboratory scientist studies the world of his specimens. I know that I should be angry, infuriated about being held captive this way, but I'm strangely calm. The rational part of me sees that there's nothing whatsoever I can do about the situation. I just wish that my head would stop hurting.

I must have fallen asleep again because my head hurts less now and the lights seem to have changed. They are a little bit brighter. I try to catch my bearings. Looking at my surroundings, I notice that there is movement outside the glass, on the side that is not covered with fake algae. People are gathering around the glass. They are staring at me. They're pointing in my direction and talking to each other, but I can't hear what they are saying. The crowd has become quite large. It's obvious that I am the show. I wonder if they expect me to do some sort of trick. I half expect someone to throw a ball, thinking that I will fetch it. This is not possible, though. As far as I can tell, the Aquarium is completely sealed, except for a door at the back, which I've just determined is locked from the other side. I'd knock, but I know that I'm on stage and my act is not yet over.

The day passes slowly. Literally thousands of people come to see me. You would think they had never seen a mermaid before. One thing is for sure: I have had a lot of time to think in my liquid cubicle. I think I've enjoyed studying these people as much as they've enjoyed studying me. Many of them are very self-conscious. They act as though they think I might know they are watching me and are embarrassed by the whole experience. I want to tell them that I understand they are curious about me; that I am also curious about them. But they wouldn't like that. They think it's okay for them to watch me, if they do so timidly. If they knew how I was appraising them, I get the feeling they would shrivel in their little spectator spots and waddle away with their tails between their legs, red-faced at their all-too-human blunder. Oddly enough, I like them for this. There's a certain sort of innocence in their feelings of undeserved guilt. Other people look at me with unabashed curiosity, as though they really would like to get inside here and feel what it's like to be me. I like them too. I wouldn't mind having legs for a day. It has a certain primal appeal.

I've been here a week and have begun to relate more and more with the people who come to watch me. I even occasionally do little swim-flips to amuse them. Mostly, I exercise at night when I am alone, except for one man who is always here when the others have gone. He watches me closely, as though he is trying to remember me from some far off time. I remember him. His nametag says, "Jake." He seems to be in a position of authority. I watch as he gives people instructions and they carry them out. He's pretty good at it. I'm learning to read lips, although I only catch bits and pieces. The hand and body gestures of these people tell me more than their lips.

Jake's beautiful blue eyes follow me everywhere I go. I swim-dance for him and I can tell that this arouses him. We seem to have a strong connection. Sometimes I think he can read my thoughts. I wonder if he knows just how tired I'm getting of living in this tiny world.

My energy seems to be waning with each passing day. I yearn for the pull of the moon, the shift of the tides. Jake watches me now with a sad look on his soulful face. Does he know what I know: That I won't live long or well in this small little world? I've learned a lot about him by watching his every movement, without any sounds to disrupt my study. I've noticed that when he is moved by something, he gets an excess of saliva in his mouth, which makes him swallow hard. His Adam's apple rises high each time this happens, as though there's not enough room in his throat for all that liquid. I have seen that he squints his eyes when he is concentrating really hard on a thought he is having. I've watched as he twists and bites his lip whenever he is impatient with a situation. He often rolls his neck to release some unseen tension. Jake walks in long, swinging strides and steps down on the front of his foot before shifting his weight to his heels. I like the way he looks and moves, legs and all. It's really too bad that there is no hope for a relationship between us. I think I could have loved him. Now, all I do is swim, around and around.

It is closing time for the show again. My act is done for another day. I look for Jake outside my window but don't see him. Too bad. He has become the high point of my life.

Suddenly, behind me there is a loud crack. The water in my cage is rushing like a strong stream toward the door in the back wall. I flow with the stream and find myself in another chamber of water. I am let through a series of doors, which I can now tell are being opened remotely by some automated system. I stay with the stream until a final door leads me out into the ocean. I look behind me and see an enormous building with a lighted sign high above it. The words read "OCEAN LIFE MUSEUM."

I swim as hard and as fast as I can, following a dim, tiny light that flickers through the water. I keep swimming until I realize that all of my efforts aren't working. The light is getting further away. I'm tired. My arms are tired and my tail is tired. I stop swimming. I need a rest. I seem to be sliding backward. the light is getting smaller and smaller. I seem to be rushing in the wrong direction. Am I really moving, or is it the light? I look for a landmark. In the distance, there is a volcano base off to my right. There was a volcano base. I guess I am moving. It's so disorienting moving backward. Maybe I should turn around. There's no light left to see this way.

I flip my tail to one side, and use my arms to right my course. That's better. At least I can see where I'm going, even if I can't control it.

I'm in some sort of current. The tow is strong. It's pulling me downward. There's a fish in front of me. He is struggling to get out, but the pressure is walling him in. It's like watching a child hit his head against the wall in the hopes that the wall will give. Should I try it? We're going deeper. How deep is too deep? It's getting harder to breath. Like being in a tunnel. Tunnel. What did Momma say about the tunnel? I can't think. The water is coming hard. It sounds like drums in my ears.

Drums...rhythm...rhythm...Tao...flow. Flow with it. Be safe.

"Okay, Karina. Calm Down. You can start by breathing." I tell myself.

I'm breathing now, but still going deeper. I'm becoming dizzy from the pressure. Very dizzy. Dizzy and tired, oh so tired. I want to keep looking to see where I'm going, but it's just too hard.

Strange. I'm in the water: In a current. Going up. I can't remember why I'm here. Did I black out? I don't know. There's a flash ahead, something white. I'm going toward it. When I reach the light, I pass into it.

I'm not in water anymore. I'm lying on a mat, surrounded by women, two middle-aged and one old. They look familiar to me. One is lifting a cup of fresh water to my mouth.

One of the middle-aged women is frowning at me. Her face is severe, as though she has spent much of her life in deep concentration on difficult subjects. I'm a little wary of her. The other middle-aged woman has a panicky set to her face. She looks as though she's accustomed to anxiety. While I'm sure she's a nice person, I'd rather not spend too much time with her. The old woman has a kind and patient face. She looks like a woman who has spent much of her life tolerating the inanity of others and has become slightly bemused by it. I keep my eyes fixed on her, avoiding the looks of the others.

"Karina," the old woman says softly. "Can you get up?"

I try to move but am very weak. "Do I have to?" I ask.

"No. Just rest. Here, have some more water." She takes the cup from the woman with the severe face and holds it to my lips.

"June, make some strong tea. Connie, go help her."

When they have left the room I ask her name. She looks at me strangely.

"I'm your Gramma," she says in a soothing tone. Then she begins to hum strange syllable sounds in low and then higher tones. I find the sound of her voice very relaxing and close my eyes.

"No, Karina. You must stay awake now. Are you hungry?" She asks.

"Hungry? No. Maybe something sweet." I say.

Gramma props me up with pillows. When the women arrive with tea, Gramma sends them back to get a dish of ice cream. In the meantime she continues to hum and tone and rub my body with a sandalwood oil. I like the earthy scent of it.

Looking around, I see candlesticks draped in hardened wax. In the centers, where candles once stood, are little silver disks and tiny bits of black string.

The severe woman and her sidekick, Ms. Panic, have come with the ice cream. Gramma is feeding it to me as though I'm a child. I have to admit that I'm enjoying the attention. The ice cream is French vanilla. It's so smooth and rich that I don't know why anyone would bother with any other food.

Out the window I can see that it's dawn. The sun is rising orange and pink. Gramma has June and Connie carry me out and set me in a lounge chair on the patio. The little house wrens are singing and flitting about. The air is a touch cool. It feels good in my lungs. I watch as the colors of the sun begin to spread their warmth into the sky.

A new day is being born and I feel like a baby, waking to see the world after a very long sleep. As the orange turns to peach and then yellow, I begin to recall the dreams I've had in these colors, dreams that seem so real. I remember the peach, the meeting of Zeus. I remember the tolerance and sympathy I felt for him. How I mastered diplomacy when the need for it went beyond my personal desires. I am most astounded by the fact that I was actually good at this. I remember yellow; seeing how my intellect overtakes my existence. And I remember learning that my body is much smarter than I imagined it was. I'm sure there was much more to these dreams, but for now it's enough that I remember them. I actually give myself credit for getting any of this, considering my initial resistance to the whole thing. Giving myself credit must be something I learned along the line too, since it is not something I normally do.

Thinking about my sea green dream makes me feel a little claustrophobic. Strange how I was imprisoned in that cubical, and how I felt compassion for the people who came to watch me. I've never liked people watching me before. Never realized what a natural thing it is. And, I remember the kind man who let me go. Jake. Jake let me go.

Gramma has come to sit next to me now. She is wiping the tears that run in those familiar little ravines on my face.

"What is it, Baby?" she asks. All I can do is bury my face in the softness of her breasts and let her rock me like an infant. I know I would have died if Jake hadn't let me go in that dream, but I can't help feeling a little unwanted.

When my river finally dries, Gramma is still holding me.

"Are you okay now, Baby?" she asks.

"Yeah. I'll be okay."

The woman with the severe face comes to stand by us.

"Hello, Momma," I say.

Gramma smiles. "She's going to be fine," she says. "But no dreamin' today. Get some sleep, everyone."

June 15

Sixth Journal Entry: Sea Green

I was a Mermaid in this journey. And Jake was my captor. It's becoming pretty clear that I have a lot of unresolved issues in my relationship with Jake.

But, what did I learn from this color? I learned that the way people interact is much more than it appears to be on the surface. The game of bantering words back and forth, always concentrating on which words you're going to form next, hides a lot of the true interaction that goes on.

I realized for the first time that I am as much a spectator of this life as a participant in it. I'm reminded of Shakespeare's "All the world is a stage and we are but actors." I think there's a separate me watching this great play we're in, and laughing at how seriously we take ourselves. I hope that I remember this the next time I'm coming completely unglued over something trivial. I also remember the current in the tunnel, how it brought me home in spite of my fighting. And how it almost didn't. I still don't understand what happened there, but I get the impression I would have weathered it better if I hadn't spent so much of my energy trying to go against it. The symbolism of Jake imprisoning me in that cubical and then releasing me is too obvious to ignore, although I wish to God I could. K.

June 15

Guide's Journal, Sixth Entry

Karina got herself captured in this color. I watched her, but couldn't penetrate the glass wall she built around herself. She watched everything from inside her protective walls. I didn't understand why she wouldn't come out, until I realized that she needed to see the world from the inside out. By inverting the thing she was having trouble with-extracting herself from the world-Karina was able to see the distinction between being of the world and being in it. I think she grasped the importance of "viewing" the world from a distance.

I could tell that Karina enjoyed her silent relationship with Jake a great deal. Maybe too much, because she stayed too long again. This time it was in an unhealthy environment. I was afraid she was not coming back to us.

When she did come back, Karina didn't recognize me, which really hurt. I felt that she did not even like me, which hurt more. I would like to be closer to her, but have trouble allowing her to be closer to me. I see the hide-and-seek game she plays with Jake being replayed with me. I wish I could say for certain that it was all Karina's doing, but I know this is a two-person game.

Karina eventually gave in to the draw of the Tao. I only hope that the action of release left enough of an imprint that she will remember it the next time the need arises. Blessed be.

When I wake up there is a telephone message pad note by my bed. My friend Jean called. She wants to know what time we're leaving for the wedding.

The wedding. I'd forgotten all about the wedding. We RSVP'd a month ago. So much has changed since then. I really don't want to go. Beth is getting married. She's a good friend and it's her first wedding. You pretty much have to go to first weddings of good friends. When it's their first wedding they really believe it's forever. And maybe it is. Maybe.

Gramma has O.K.'d my going to the wedding and reception.

"Having a lot of contact with people will do you good," she said. I didn't quite understand that.

The wedding goes off like pretty much every other wedding I have ever attended. Beth has a large family and they are all in the party. I hate the hand shaking part. How many different ways are there to say, "It was a beautiful wedding. That bride's maid gown is very flattering, really."

The reception is another story. We are in a large hall. The caterer is family and has filled us with more than is decent for a body to eat. I'm also imbibing my share of the fruit of the vine. Jean has taken an interest in a muscle-bound Swede. But I don't care. The band is great, and I'm happy to be absorbing their rhythms. They are playing songs that I know for a change. Who'd have thought that at twenty-nine my tastes would be out of style?

Jake is here. He has spent most of the evening on the dance floor. I'm trying not to look, but I've noticed that the girls are asking him to dance. These are people who pretend to be my friends. The corpse of our relationship is hardly cold in the ground, and like old maids fighting over the last sperm in town, they claw and climb over each other at the beginning of each song to get to him first. Some of them have looked my way, but none have made eye contact.

This same tacky guy keeps asking me to dance. He's a relative of Beth's from out of state somewhere. I tell him and a few others that I'm not in a dancing mood tonight. Instead I sit and watch my Ex float across the floor with varying shades of blond and brown. No red heads yet.

Walking to the bar to get another glass of wine, Jake intercepts me.

"Dance with me," he says.

"I'm not in the mood," I pout.

"Please. I can't take much more small talk and innuendo."

"All right." I take pity on him. "But then you buy me a drink."

"You got it."

We make our way to the dance floor, and I can swear I feel daggers shooting from surrounding tables, but I don't look.

"I didn't expect to see you here," he says. I thought you'd be...busy."

He's being careful not to say the words, and I appreciate his attempt, clumsy as it may be.

"I'm taking a night off."

"I didn't know you could do that."

"It was Gramma's call."

"Is something wrong?" he asks. "Are you all right?" He actually sounds very concerned.

"I'm all right." I say. And that is all I'm saying.

The band begins to play Color My World, which used to be our song. Jake continues to hold me and press me with the sway of his hard body. Choking back a tear, I swallow my pain and try to think about tomorrow's journey... mocha almond fudge ice cream... a new outfit I've had my eye on...anything but this moment. He's let me go twice now, one the divorce and two in the aquarium. But that wasn't real, or was it? Either way, I'm not about to step up to the bat for number three.

"I'm sorry about the restaurant." He says.

"Let's not talk about it."

"Ya know," he says, "sometimes I wish we'd had children. I think that would have made a difference."

When he says this, I get a pain in the area of my left ovary: a twinge of regret. Most people shouldn't have children just to keep a relationship together, but with Jake and I it might have worked. Of course, we'd probably still be miserable, but we'd be together.

"I really have to go now," I tell him. "I have a big day tomorrow." Prying myself away from him is not easy, but neither is staying.

"Karina, be careful," he says. Then he smiles.

"You too," I say, giving him my best not-quite-smile smile.

June 16

Seventh Journal Entry: No Color

Today I had a day off from journeying. Instead, I went to a wedding reception, which almost felt like a journey, a journey to another time. Jake was there and we danced. I shouldn't have done that. K.

June 16

Guide's Journal, Seventh Entry

Karina had the day off, because of her close call yesterday. I watched her as she came in from her night out. Her thoughts still seem to be on something distant and unhappy. I will light an extra candle tonight, holding my intention that Karina will be safe during tomorrow's journey. She is going farther into the colors than I expected she would. If she survives, this will be very good for her. Blessed be.

Chapter Seven - Green
Holding Healing

Momma is looking distant, but not in her usual "Drill-Sergeant-isolating-herself-from-a new-recruit" way. Today her distance has a melancholy tone, almost like a lover afraid of being betrayed. We're not a real touchy-feely family, but I go over and give her a hug. I may need this hug as much as she does.

Momma has prepared my bath water, and I languish in the embrace of the warm, silky liquid around my body. The scent of rose oil is strong today. The frankincense is burning. My mind is already beginning to get in the mode for travel to color-land. Habits have always come easily to me; it's breaking them I can't bear.

I am in my black journey robe and the room is ready. I notice that the candles are taller and wider than usual. I guess it really isn't good if they go out.

"Karina," Momma says, "you know that I'm here if you need me."

Momma's been very nice to me, ever since the sea green dream. Maybe she thought I wasn't going to come back.

"I know, Momma," I say.

"Karina, about the tunnel. I know I've been telling you not to touch it. I still don't want you to touch it, but this time I do want you to feel it."

"How can I feel it without touching it?" I ask.

"I want you to feel it with your mind and with your energy. Just think very hard about the tunnel's energy while you are in it."

"I'll try," I say.

Momma hands me the Goddess; and I begin my rhyme to the color green.

"Flow-er of vibrancy
blowing like grass
tall and wild,
hiding the past.
Seep into spaces
holding dis-ease
healing and lifting
memory
from knees
scabbed and scarred,
oozing with pain.
Cleanse me thoroughly,
Green energy, rain."

I'm sitting at a table that is only inches from the floor. A white-faced woman in a kimono is pouring green tea into two small, round cups set in front of me. She pours only a small amount in one and fills the other half way.

"Drink this one first," she says. She hands me the one with only a splash in it. I drink, trying to avoid the herbs that have settled on the bottom.

She picks up the cup and half-closes her eyes to help her concentrate on the tea leafs.

"You are going on a journey to a far-off place," she says.

"Yes, I know," I say.

"Have a pleasant journey," she says.

"Thank you." I look at the other cup. I move my face close to it, and breath in the richness of the cha. I hold the cup in my hand and toast her. "To my journey," I say.

I'm walking through tangan-tangan trees, into a jungle. The overgrown, twisting and intertwining trunks of the tangan-tangan are fighting the long palm fronds of the coconut trees for space. There are exotic ferns growing in between razor sharp blades of thick and standing grass. Brown patches peek through foliage covering an old path. I listen for clues as to which way to go. Between the caw of the Macaw and the chirping of insects, I hear the sound of rushing water and feel my body stretch to move in its direction.

My body feels limber, although I haven't been exercising it lately. Or have I? I can't remember

I reach the water, expecting pools of blue, but instead the stream is a flowing field of emerald green. There is a man-made pond of the liquid off to the side of the main rush of water. A narrow hose that is mostly - but not completely - covered by dirt feeds it. I lean over to get a better look at the emerald liquid. I catch my breath as I see my face reflecting up from the endless depth of this color. I make a fashion note to myself to buy something in emerald green. My face is vibrating with life. Actually, everything around me is vibrating in a queer way. I can sense the sentience of the trees and the grass.

"Where in the world am I?" I ask out loud.

"You are at the center of the universe," a voice replies from behind me. I turn and see a gentle-faced woman. She has a kind face with soft gray hair, and bright blue-green eyes. The skin around her eyes folds gently, as though it's kneeling in reverence to the power of the force radiating from them. I sense immediately that she is a woman who has lived a long time and hasn't wasted any of the lessons she's learned along the way.

"Where, exactly, is the center of the universe?"

"You're about to find out," she says. "Follow me."

I'm not sure I really want to know where the center of the universe is, but I don't know where else to go, so I follow her. We climb a steep path that rises up the side of the mountain.

"Deer and wild boar," she says, pointing at the path. The old woman is quite nimble and keeping a pretty good pace. When we get to the top, I'm breathing heavily. I look at her closely, but can see no sign that she has just climbed about one hundred feet at the rate of a triathlon power-walker.

Reaching a plateau, we stop. Rich vegetation flourishes all around us. She bends over and picks a leave.

"Squaw vine," she says. "I'll make you a tea of it. It will help."

"Help what?"

"Your problem, Dear." She looks at me as though I'm a piece of cloth she is inspecting for flaws. "Your woman problem."

I want to ask her how she can tell, but know that it will only make me look foolish. She can tell because she can tell, like Gramma.

We follow a path for a few yards that leads straight to the door of her home. It's a dome-shaped building made of dried mud bricks, dyed the green of the surrounding foliage. Thick vines are strung across the ceiling. Hanging from them is every herb known to woman. There are other women living in this dome. I look, but don't see any men. Some of the women are cooking something that smells to me like marijuana in large steel pots. All of the women are humming various one-syllable mantras.

I look around and notice that in each of the windows is a prism. On the opposite walls are spectrum rows, each color sliding perfectly into the one before and after it. Seeing the rainbows, I begin to relax a little, despite myself. I don't want to let my guard down. I've learned that people who seem nice can turn instantly if they feel their space has been threatened, like black bears protecting a cub. I definitely feel out of my league here.

"Please have a seat." The old woman gestures at a pillow in the center of a sunken space in the floor.

I go to the pillow and sit. One by one the other women follow me into the sunken space. They are wearing hooded cloaks. The hoods are large and cover most of their faces. They sit without pillows, circling me. Their humming is directed at me now. It's making me edgy. They are all placing their hands on me.

"Drink this." The old woman is holding a cup to my lips. It's the spiced herb drink that I think may be a hallucinogen.

I hesitate and she lifts the cup, pouring a little on my chin. Some slipped through my lips and onto my tongue. The taste is rich and sensuous, so I drink more. Reaching for the cup myself, I see why she's holding it for me. My hands are trembling. The woman reaches her left hand to touch my right one and I'm instantly calmed.

I look into the depths of her eyes and they penetrate into the abyss of mine. I cannot remove myself from their hold.

"Relax, my Dear," she says. "The Green Mother is waking in you and soon you will be one with her. There is no point in fighting."

"I don't want anyone waking in me."

There is a collective gasp from the women around me. The humming stops. I'm guessing that was not the right thing to say.

"But you requested this, in your rhyme. Listen to your heart. You cannot fight the Green Mother now. You are she. The battle is within. We can see you are used to fighting yourself. From now on you must be more careful. You have more power, and your wounds could be greater."

The humming starts again, and the hands come back. In spite of all the women around me, I feel desperately alone: A stranger in a foreign land. I glance at the women. Behind one of the hoods, I see a face that looks familiar. The shape of the face is uncannily like Momma's. For a second, I catch her eyes. I'm sure it is Momma, but she looks away. The energy emanating from the hands becomes strong. I feel a warm sensation burning the inside of me. Instinctively, I close my eyes to try to find it. My vision is filled with a green light. It starts inside my body and extends beyond it. Like the dancing glitter of birthday sparkles, it fills the air around me.

I realize that I'm still resisting. My body is tense. "Relax, it's okay," I tell my muscles. The dancing sparkles begin to swirl into a cone-shaped funnel. On the walls of the funnel, I see myself:

As a little girl-stealing a blouse from a department store. I am ashamed that I did that, and feel a sharp pain in my right hip...In an evening scene where Momma is interrogating me. I had come home late. I feel myself getting angry with her. Harsh words. "Why would I come home to a woman who isn't even available when she is there?" I feel the muscles in my neck contract into a spasm. I cannot breathe...Acting stupidly jealous in a recurring scene with Jake, and feel a wrenching throb in my chest...Scene after scene goes by and I am one huge bundle of shooting pain and aching muscles. I just can't hold all of this hurt. I'm going to burst. I'm going to die.

Just as this thought enters my mind, the heat begins to take over.

As if in a trance, I hear a faraway voice say, "The first step to healing is to release your past, Karina. Find the now moment and forgive in it. The forgiveness will vibrate back in time."

The women still have their hands on me. One by one they begin to pull them away. As the energy of their hands passes from me, I start to feel weak and dizzy. When there is only one pair of hands left on me, I pass out.

Everything is dark. I smell the earthy scent of moss. The air feels moist and clammy. I'm walking through something that feels like the inside of a huge, dead tree. I'm trying to focus on what is around me, but everything is so dark.

I'm trying to walk quickly, but I don't want to stumble. I wish I could see. I close my eyes and try to remember a light. When I open them again, there is a small flame at the end of the tree. I realize that I am in the tunnel.

"Feel it," I hear Momma saying.

Stopping for a moment, I let my consciousness crawl toward the walls. Even so, I bump against it. The sensation strikes me brutally. It feels like the hollow aching of a life that is being sucked back in on itself. How unbearably typical, I think. These walls are made of the mind-set I live most of the time, but without the haze of denial to dilute them, the reality of their pain is piercingly plain to perceive.

I begin to walk toward the flame. As I get closer, I begin to worry. What if it's not just for light? What if it's for burning? I'm supposed to stay away from the fire. I know that. But I need the light. I know that too. I decide that if it's a controlled flame, like a gas lamp, then it's not really a fire.

I keep watching it too afraid to go forward, in case it's the wrong thing to do. What if the light changes?

Too drained by the pain of my own redundancy to go back, I've been standing here what seems like a very long time. Since the light hasn't spread, it must be controlled. I'm relieved to have worked this out. I begin walking again.

When I reach the flame, it changes form. The light disperses and all that is left is a glow in the air. I walk through it.

I am lying in the journey room with Momma bending over me, her hands on my heart.

"How do you feel, Honey?" Momma asks.

"Fine." I mentally check the various parts of my body to make sure that I'm not lying. "Just fine."

"Good," she says. "You weren't gone too long. Some people take much longer in this color."

I look around the room. The candles are only half burnt. "It was long enough, I say. The women didn't waste any time with me." Momma smiles a knowing grin.

"Do you want to talk about it?" she asks. I remember seeing her in the dream.

"Were you there?" I ask.

"Did you see me?" she asks.

"Yes. I'm pretty sure I did."

"Then I was there," she says.

"But how, Momma, how did you get into my dream?"

"Well, you haven't been alone in these dreams. They've always included other people, haven't they?"

"You're doing it again." I say. "You're not answering my question."

"All right. I'll try." She looks at me for a moment. "In school you studied Carl Jung?" she asks.

"Yes."

"So, you're familiar with his theory of the collective unconscious? That at some level there is a consciousness we all share?"

"You're saying that I've been traveling to the collective unconscious?" I ask.

"I'm saying that, like Jung's collective unconscious, you've been traveling to a dimension that is available to anyone."

"Well then, what about the tunnel? Why do I have to travel through the tunnel alone?" I ask.

"Carl Jung had a good model to explain this. He said that if you are the house, your unconscious is the basement. Inside the basement, there is a trap door that leads to the collective unconscious," Momma says.

"I believe that, although we are going to the same place, we must each enter through and learn to control our own trap door."

"Wow," I say. "I have to admit that I'm a little amazed. This actually makes some kind of sense."

"Well, I'm glad that you get it. I think that's enough for you to think about for now. Later, we'll talk more. By the way, how was the tunnel?"

"The tunnel? Oh, dark and dying. It smelled of moss and felt like compost."

"Compost is good," she said. "Compost is the end of an old life and the beginning of new one."

"Yeah, well, I'd like to begin with some food. I'm starved."

"Gramma's been cooking her secret red sauce," she says. "I'll tell her you're back so she can put on the pasta. It'll only take a minute.

This traveling sure burns up calories.

As we eat, I'm aware of Gramma staring at me. She looks at me in the same way the old woman in the dream did. I can't help wondering if they are related. Maybe the woman was a dead relative of the family coven? No, couldn't be. Could it?

"Thanks for the great dinner, Gramma," I say. "I'm going to go write in my journal now."

"I think I'll do the same," says Momma. "If no one minds."

"You go ahead, June. We'll take care of everything," Gramma says.

It's an innocent enough sentence, but I find myself wondering what "everything" is.

⁘ ⁘ ⁘

June 17

Eighth Journal Entry: Emerald Green

> *I was astounded to feel the amount of memories I carry in my body as pain. The pain was animated, with a knowing intelligence I hadn't even seen living inside the rest of my consciousness. I feel I've been hosting a party without realizing that I had unruly, unwelcome guests influencing the tone and tempo of the rest of the group. What's worse, these lively, emotional beings actually took up residence when I wasn't looking. It's sad to grasp that I've spent my whole life not looking.*

> *Coming to forgiveness is even harder. I'm not really great at forgiving other people, but I'm absolutely worst at forgiving myself. I had blocked most of those memories out of my mind, or never considered them much to begin with. I guess my*

body hadn't forgotten. Chalk up one more point for its
intelligence. I see more clearly now the lesson of
yellow prepared me for green. I guess Momma is
right. The journeys do build on each other.

I also learned that I'm more stubborn than I
realized. Even though I knew the women were trying
to help me, I didn't want them to touch me. It's almost
as though I felt I didn't deserve the love they were
pouring into me, or that I couldn't accept all that
positive energy inside me. This is not something one
likes to face about oneself.

I know I've done a lot of things wrong in my
life, but those women didn't care. And once they loved
me, my body stopped caring too. She just responded.
She opened up to start the healing process. Maybe
love is the great healer, after all.

On some level, I knew that Momma was
taking this journey with me all along, but since I
didn't actually see her, I could kind of ignore her
presence. I perceive now that I ignore almost all the
things that I cannot directly see. I hope I get to see
and understand more of Momma. Much of her life still
remains a mystery. K.

June 17

Guide's Journal, Eighth Entry

Karina got through the lesson on healing
quite quickly. This was the color I was most
worried about. It seems I don't know as much
about my daughter as I thought I did. The Wise
Women sat her down and healed her without

interrogation. I have never seen this happen before. Something inside her must have led them to it. In spite of her outward arrogance, Karina is meek at the core.

I was touched to feel Karina's pain for our relationship, and saddened to think I had contributed to it. I should probably visit this color again soon myself. There is a lot I can learn by watching Karina.

I was pleased with the way she accepted witnessing my inter-dimensional travel. I hadn't told her about it before because I was afraid she wouldn't want to go if she thought I was there with her. Even as a child, Karina wanted to learn everything herself. I still wonder if one of her reasons for taking this journey wasn't to get away from me. I hope knowing I'm there doesn't negatively influence her will to continue.

Thank the Goddess that Karina passed well through this color. I'm glad to know that the Wise Women like her. Blessed be.

I'm up early and can't get back to sleep. Actually, I feel really good. I've decided to go for an early morning jog in the park. I usually avoid jogging in the park this time of day because I know this is when Jake jogs. He'll probably think I'm trying to see him. Guys think that way, especially police guys. Always on the chase. But I don't care. I want to jog in the park, and I won't be scared away from the things I want to do because of what someone else thinks anymore. God, I sound like my mother.

The fresh morning air is splashing my skin and I'm glad I decided to come here. The air is so much richer among the trees. There's someone jogging toward me from a ways down the path. Thanks to Jake, even in all this beauty I'm aware that I have to stay alert for perverts and muggers. As he gets closer I can see that it's the man I passed the other afternoon. The one I had that strange vision of, with Anne. As he passes me, it happens again. This time I see them in wedding clothes. It's a full color flash, right out of virtual reality. I turn around to take another look at him, and he's looking back at me. He's looping around and jogging toward me.

"Excuse me," he says. "This may sound strange. I just got a strong feeling that I should talk to you. Do I know you?"

"No. But I think you know, or should know, someone I know. This sounds pretty stupid, I'm sure. But I just had a sort of intuition, or something. It happened the last time I saw you too."

We are both still running in place to keep our muscles warm.

"Do you know Anne Calloway?"

"No. I don't think so."

"Well, I think you should meet. But I can't give you her number. Especially since I don't know you. Do you want to give me yours?"

"Well, yes. I'm just divorced. Yeah. I'd like to meet someone nice. I'm Bob, by the way."

"Bob. I'm Karina."

"Here," he says, pulling something from his pocket. "I suppose it seems strange. Carrying a business card when you're jogging. It's just I'm in sales, and you never know."

We both turn to continue our jogs when I notice another jogger coming down the path. He's close enough for me to see that it's Jake. I wonder why I didn't hear him sooner. Realizing that he must have seen Bob give me his card, I immediately feel like a kid getting caught with candy in school.

He slows down as he gets close to me. He turns to jog beside me.

"Hi." I say, and keep jogging like nothing happened. Which nothing did.

"Who was that?"

"Oh, just a guy I met. Bob."

"Are you in the habit of talking to strange men in the park?" I turn to look at him now. He isn't even breathing hard. He could at least get winded when he runs, like a normal person.

"No. Actually, I'm not," I tell him.

"What did he want?"

"What is this, the Spanish inquisition? I met him. We talked. There's no law against that, is there, Officer?"

"Not if that's all that happens."

I can feel the blood inside me rise toward my head, which I know from experience means I will lose control. "How can you expect me to be your friend when you jump down my throat every chance you get?" It comes out in stuttered gasps, since my breathing rhythm is now completely erratic.

"Karina, I'm just looking out for you. I want you to realize that not everyone deserves your trust. There are bad people out there, with very bad intentions." Jake reaches his hand and fingers my face as he says this. The tenderness of his touch is excruciating.

"It's the ones with good intentions that really hurt you."

I see him wince as he retracts and know that I have once again wounded him.

"Thanks, Karina. Thanks a lot."

Jake turns and runs in the other direction.

I can't believe my own witlessness. "Nice going, Karina. Real nice."

Chapter Eight - Teal
A Future Found

The pedal-soft scant of rose rises with the steam that surrounds me, while the layer of liquid that clings closest to my skin silkens it with molecules gathered so closely that they form a film, delicately protecting all that is inside me from all that is out. I feel blessed to have my new shield defending me from the elements of life. If knowledge is power, then understanding is protection. I may not comprehend everything yet, but I feel stronger for the things I do get.

Absorbing the warmth of the moment, I can't help thinking that I've learned a lot about myself on this journey, but nothing that explains why I can't get along with Jake. When we were first dating I thought it was adorable how he always wanted to protect me. I actually loved having someone who cared enough to do that. My Dad and Momma divorced when I was four and I never got over the feeling that he left because he didn't want me. Momma always said that he was still my father and still her husband - that two souls that had once been joined would always share a part of each other.

Maybe that's why I can't let go of Jake. The echoes of Momma's beliefs haunt me. Maybe we really are one. Or maybe it's all a crock and I'm going to end up as cold and lonely as Momma seems to be for no good reason. I wish there was a way to know these things for sure, to peek into the secret cosmos I'm learning really does exist, to sit a while with the angels and ask them to teach me.

"Karina." Momma says. "It's time to begin."

I roll over onto my belly and dunk my face in the water, blowing out the air of frustration left inside my brain. I want to be clear-headed and ready for this color: teal. It is one of my favorites in the rainbow.

The Goddess is on her mat, waiting for me. She seems so real at times that I half expect her to reach out and touch me, before the journey starts. Momma says I can ask her questions, and that I will get my answers if I listen carefully. Momma also tells me to meditate on my dreams at night. So far, I have not had much luck with those.

"Karina, before you begin, I want you to remember that things are not always what they seem to be."

"Please Momma, if you're going to give me advice at the last minute, try to be a little more concrete," I say. I know that Momma has trouble with reality, but what am I supposed to do with 'things are not what they seem'?

"The world is not always as orderly as it seems," she tries. "There are quirks in the system. Some things happen in ways that no one understands, and that is natural. It's called synchronicity."

"I'm glad you cleared that up," I say, shaking my head. Sometimes I wonder why I ask.

"And remember," she says, "to feel the tunnel. But not with your body."

"Do I have to?" I ask, knowing the answer. Remembering the pain of the last tunnel experience, I'm reluctant. Yet, afterward, there was that welcome release.

Momma doesn't answer.

I pick up the Goddess and begin my rhyme to teal.

"Flasher of insights
a future unfolds
mechanical moments
are stories untold

And maybe unlived.
Ideally, or not
What's coming remembered
what's past now forgot.

Shifter of seconds

Rainbow Goddess: A Journey Tale

*traveling rhyme,
release to me moments
rifting through time."*

I'm in a gymnasium inside a school. There's a man in a T-shirt and sweats blowing a whistle. All of the girls on the floor stop, except for one. She shoots the basketball through the hoop in one last attempt to get points. The ball swishes through a green-blue net. The girl turns. She is wearing a baggy sack of teal that the school calls a uniform. She winks at me. As she runs by me, she slaps my but.

"Come on. Let's get a drink." She says.

I follow her to the drinking fountain. It's closer to the floor than I remember. She drinks first. I watch her swallow the blue-green liquid.

"Mmm. This tastes like fun. To your journey." She says.

I bend over and take my swish. "To my journey."

My lab is filled with electronic equipment: cathode ray oscilloscopes and variations on these. Some are attached to computers with luminous graphs flashing all over the screens. There are atomic clocks, and more computers. The computer screens are all colored teal. They cast a low-level, mood-setting glow on the room when I shut off the overhead lights. I do this when I need to think, which is often. I'm very close to a breakthrough. I think the prototype is perfect. If only I can find the right frequency. The right wave length. The right vibrational space between waves of light and moments of time.

I am looking for "rider" frequencies flowing within known ones, or a frequency above or below those currently harnessed or realized. I am looking for the short-cut psychics take through time to see the future. I have researched and tested every willing psychic I could find, trying to find the link that leads them into future events. I theorize that somewhere in this questioning is where I will find my ultimate goal. I am searching for the impulse that moves continually through the universe, Newton's perpetual motion come subatomic, skipping through space with enough energy to fuel the world. I have isolated it down to a band that is still incomprehensibly large.

The prototype is shaped like a geode. When I find the impulse I am looking for, it will channel into a hole on one side, pass through the sensor/amplifier and release out the other end onto a photovoltaic grid. I'd better hit on something soon, because my grant is running out, and no one really believes in my project, except Jake. Even he may only be supporting me because he loves me.

It's been a long week. I'm almost ready to let myself take a little nap. I'll just check the prototype one more time.

"Holy mothers!" The geode is lit. The grid is glowing like the sun!

"Holy mothers!" I've hit pay dirt. Well, pay waves. Actually, free waves. I've discovered free energy. I knew it. Ever since I read Einstein's theory of time variance I've known that there was energy transferring in the spaces between time. If we could just find that energy and magnify it, we wouldn't need to burn fossil fuel. We wouldn't need to create nuclear waste. We wouldn't need to run wires across cities or under ground. We could just leave the Earth to the Earth, which, at this point in time, would be a very good thing. The Earth is in a pretty desperate state.

I look over at the photo grid. It's so bright. I'm amazed that it isn't overloading.

I need to call Jake.

The phone rings one, two, three times.

"Come on. Come on. Pick up!" My heart is racing, my fingers jerking in their sockets. I can't keep my mind from whirling in large, concentric circles.

"Hello."

"Jake. Jake. I've done it. I found it. I found the frequency. It's working."

"Whoa, whoa, whoa! Karina. Listen to me. I hear you. And I'm excited for you. But we have to get off the phone. Right now. This phone could be tapped. Please don't say anything more. I'll be right over."

He'll be right over. He's excited for me. How about: He's excited for the world?

I swear. Sometimes that man is so paranoid that it makes me want to scream. It's not bad enough that I have to do all my on-line interfacing on a separate computer. That I have to have my work-in-progress computer so encrypted that half of the time I can't follow what I've done. It's not enough that he won't let me publish papers on my work-to-date for fear I'll become some type of espionage target. Now, he can't even say "congratulations!" on the phone.

I know he's naturally suspicious. It's that early police force training, and now his years as a government Secret Service Agent. Still, you'd think it would be enough that he checks my phone every time he's here. He talked the institute into insisting that I put a state-of-the-art security system in my lab. I'm here all the time. When does he think someone is going to break in?

"Karina?" Jake calls out.

It's a good thing he has the alarm code, because I'm not sure I would let him in right now. Yes, I would, if I could get my hands to cooperate. I have to show someone this beautiful, glowing grid of energy. It's a very unusual color. The light seems to be vibrating. I may be losing my mind, but I actually seem to feel more alive when I stand near it.

"Jake, come here. Look at this."

"Jesus, Karina. You did do it."

"I told you I did." I say.

"Do you know what this means?" Jake asks.

"Yeah. It means free energy for the entire world. One time purchases and lifetime lights. Except maybe a little sensor repair now and then. I'm going to take my profits from the set-up sales and buy gens- I think I'm going to just call them "gens"- for placement in third world schools and hospitals. It'll really be a New Age."

"Yeah. The first step to Utopia."

Jake brushes his lips across the tips of mine. I love that feathery feeling. He wraps his arms around my shoulders and moves them slowly down my back, resting them on my softness. There is so much energy in the room. I feel heightened in every way. Is it the orb, or the thrill of victory? It doesn't matter. All I can think of right now is getting to the pinnacle of pleasure. I decide not to stop his hands from roaming further, from unbuttoning, unzipping, from caressing.

I look up at Jake and see a halo of light surrounding his body, pulsing, pushing its way into the space of energy between us. He appears so much like all the Gods I've ever imagined, rolled into one wonderful scrumptious, supernatural being. My hand, now a model of graceful fluidity, reaches toward him. His hand waltzes up to welcome mine. All becomes one as we merge into the lifting, shifting, escalating and cascading energy that entwines us. We let ourselves fall under its stimulating spell.

We've made love in this room before, even used this table, but it never, ever felt this wonderful. Soaking up the stray vibrations we hadn't quite harnessed in our urge to merge with the eternal wow, we lay content.

"Mmm." I say. "You really know how to throw a celebration."

"Not so bad yourself."

I love the way he holds me when we're done. His arms are so strong and protective. He's my private bodyguard, which is nice to have. Even if all the villains are imaginary.

"Remind me to put a sensor and a large heating pad on this table," I say.

"It does get cold quickly," he rolls over and offers me his hand, this time in a steadying way.

We both stand up and begin gathering our clothes.

"Now, Karina, I know you don't want to hear this, but there are precautions you're going to have to take. First of all, where have you recorded the frequency?"

"Dear Goddess! I haven't. I've just been mesmerized by the thing."

"Do it now, but only in your coded computer. And then do a back up onto a new disk. Make two copies. We'll run them to make sure they formatted okay. And then we'll erase your hard drives."

"Are you crazy? Look, Jake, I know you're really into this espionage thing, but don't you think you're taking it a bit far?"

"Absolutely not. Do you have any idea what this is going to do to the world economy? I know that you think it's going to be the great equalizer. But not everybody wants to be equalized. Whole corporations will go bankrupt. Thousands, maybe millions of stockholders will lose their shirts. Entire countries will suddenly have no bargaining power. Countries whose central God is power. And some people who can't even think that far will be really pissed off. All they are going to know is that now they are out of a job. This is big time, Karina."

"Goddess. I hadn't thought of any of that. I was so wrapped up in the space-time transference thing."

"That's another thing. If you let the theory behind this loose, it opens a crack in the door to time travel. Capturing this frequency may not be a one-way ride."

"Shit."

"Listen. Let's just do what we can to protect this and then we'll go to the diner for some java and make a game plan," he says.

"Shit."

"Karina. Come on. You have to record that frequency and then deselect it on the sphere. We're going to put that and one of the disks in the safe. The back up I'm going to store someplace special."

I do as I'm told, my head still spinning with the possibility that Jake may, for once, be right. I'm actually beginning to sway with dizziness. How long has it been since I've eaten, I wonder?

The diner is a "greasy spoon," but they have the best apple pie in town.

"Where are you going to store the other disk?" I ask Jake.

He writes his answer on a piece of paper. It reads: In my Grandmother's safety deposit box, under her alias. His Grandmother was paranoid too.

"But," I say.

"Shhh," he says, and hands me the pen.

But she is dead. I write.

"That's the beauty of it. No one knows about it but me." He burns the paper we wrote on. The waitress is giving us a look.

"Here," he says, passing me a list. "I knew that you wouldn't be thinking about it, so I did some background checks on manufacturing firms and an attorney. I think you should get in touch with this guy first thing in the morning."

"So, you really did believe I was going to do it?"

"Of course. I told you I did."

"I know. I'm just really glad to know that you took me seriously."

The rush of adrenaline and whatever else was thrusting me on has taken its very stiff toll. I'm so tired. All I want now is to sleep. I'm tempted to go back and sleep in the lab, absorbing all that wonderful air, but the orb is locked away and I do not want to argue with Jake to release it.

I've overslept. It's nearly noon. Wow. I haven't slept like this since I don't know when. It's like I was knocked out or something. Finding a form of energy that will change the world must be some kind of sedative, or maybe it was that energy. It was unlike anything I've ever felt before.

The phone is ringing. It's probably Jake.

"Hello," I say.

"Listen carefully. If you ever want to see your pretty boyfriend again, you'll do as I say. I want both copies of the disk delivered to me or he's a dead man. And the orb, don't forget that. Don't bother making any more copies of the disk, either, because I'll be watching you. Meet us at ten o'clock tonight at the Science Museum. And don't try to contact anyone. This is a private matter." Click. The receiver is silent. Can it be true? Do they have Jake? Who are they?

I try to call Jake's apartment and there's no answer. I call his beeper and leave my number.

Someone is answering.

"Jake?"

"Do you believe me now?" The voice asks. "Nice try, but the beeper came with the man. You'd better do as I say, if you ever want to see your sweetheart again." Click.

"Shit." What do I do now? What are my choices? I can save Jake. Or I can save the planet. I can have love, or I can have a New World, but not both. Why is it never both? I have to think. Why can't I think?

"What do they want? That is the first question." I say out loud, even though no one is listening. Or maybe someone is. Shit! Creepy. They're probably watching me now. I look around the room, but have no idea what I'm looking for. Nothing looks obviously like a camera. I get a blanket and cover my television. Jake says it's like a two-way mirror. I can see the world, but the world can also see me, with the right technology.

And all this time I thought he was just paranoid.

It's four o'clock and I'm in my lab. The teal lights that are usually so soothing are really beginning to irritate me. Anyway, I'm covering the machines as a precaution. I've taken the sphere and the disk out of the safe.

Now I have to decide. Do I destroy them? Do I hand them over? Do I bring them to the attorney and have him start the patenting process? Do I go to the police?

If I'm really being watched, everything - except handing them over - will get Jake killed. Also, there's the other problem. I don't have any idea what his grandmother's alias was, or in which bank she might have her box. Pretty much, I'm screwed.

I'm feeling faint. I need to eat. I uncover one of my computers and order from my favorite Chinese restaurant. I order from Wong's a lot, so I find it easily on the Internet. It's hard to get through on the phone. Wong told me in confidence that he fills his computer orders first. He hates the phone. Says people are always getting their numbers mixed up, ordering the wrong meal and then blaming it on Wong. He does all his advertising on the Internet; has it programmed up so that the messages hit the local bulletin boards just before lunch and just before dinner.

That's it! Why didn't I think of that? Time-loaded messages. I can load the disk into the computer and have it set to play at midnight, just in case they won't want to release Jake. Or, in case they kill us both. Better not think of that.

I'll send it to every university science department listed, to Environmental Causes bulletin boards and to all the law enforcement people Jake knows. If I do make it back in time, I can erase the message before it's sent. Okay, this works. This way they'll have an incentive to release us. The last thing they want is the specs on this project broadcast around the world. And if we do die, at least it will have been for a good cause, although this is not a comforting notion.

It's ten o'clock. The entrance to the museum is unlocked, but no lights are on inside. I still don't have the other disk, but I made a copy of the one I had. Something smells funny in here. Like, I don't know what, maybe gas.

"Jake!" I shout. "Are you here?"

I hear an urging voice in the back of my mind.

"Karina. Karina." The voice is Momma's.

Damn. I forgot I was supposed to call Momma. It seems urgent I call her. I go to the pay phone just outside the door and dial her.

"Come home right away." She says. An explosion shakes the building, and I feel myself being pulled through a vortex in the phone line.

The walls of the vortex keep moving in and out, becoming clear and then fuzzy. I remember Momma saying to feel the tunnel. I close my eyes. It's so disorienting. It's almost like the tunnel is a pulse and I can feel its heartbeat. First it is fast, and then it is really slow. I open my eyes. It's fast when it is clear and slow when it is fuzzy. The opposite of film, I think. Strange. It's fast when it's in and slow when it's out. I can't seem to get its rhythm. Maybe there is none. I reject that theory. There must be a rhythm.

How can I walk through it if I don't know when to go fast and when to go slow? I just keep marching along, keeping pace as best I can.

I see a light. It's far away and fuzzy. It's taking me a really long time to get there. I keep going. I feel like I'm not getting any nearer the light.

No. Wait, now it's clear and close. I can almost touch it.

The walls waffle and it becomes far again. No. Come back. I want clear and close. I want fast. I want everything over now, but I don't know why. The walls shift again. The light is almost on me. I run toward it.

Lying flat on my back, I hear Momma singing a low, sad song.

"Am I really here?" I ask. "What happened to Jake?"

"Wasn't he with you?"

"Yes. Umm, in the dream."

"Well, then you already know."

"Momma, if someone is hurt in a dream, are they hurt? I mean, does it really affect them in real life, even if it wasn't their dream?"

"Dreams are real, Karina. They are just different dimensions. No one knows how what takes place in one dimension of reality affects what happens in another. There are many dimensions, many realities. The knowledge we gain by moving through a dimension can influence us in all of them. But no single dimension is any more real than another. I thought you understood that."

"Life was so much simpler before it had all these dimensions and energies. I'm a little overwhelmed by the thought of it all," I say.

"Karina, we've been practicing our rituals year after year. What did you think they meant?"

"Well, metaphors. I thought they were all metaphors, like stories out of Greek mythology or something."

"How was the tunnel?" she asks.

"It was weird. It had a heartbeat. And a pulse. It shifted."

"You felt it well," Momma said. High praise from Momma, I think. But I'm still worried about Jake.

"I didn't like it."

"You have a lot to learn, Karina." Momma looks into my eyes. "You're obviously upset. I think you should spend some time meditating."

"Yeah, and finding Jake," I whisper.

Jake will be at work now. Cruising the city in a car with red and blue lights on the top. It'll be the middle of the morning before he's home. I could leave a message for him, but it's technically not an emergency; and I can just imagine the flack he'd get from the boys about his ex-wife calling. I'll go jogging early and look for him in the park. I don't have to talk to him. Just see if he's okay.

"Spicy lentil soup," Gramma announces. "Fresh baked peach pie for desert."

Just in time. I'm starved.

❖ ❖ ❖

June 18

Ninth Journal Entry: Teal

> *In this color, I invented a way to harness the fluctuations of time's energy. What a concept! What's so strange is how real and logical it all seemed to me at the time.*
>
> *Jake and I made love on a table, with scads of vibrations dancing through us. That was pretty phenomenal. (Not that making love with Jake in this dimension isn't unspeakably satisfying.) There was something really incredible about the energy of that time-frequency. I wonder if there is such a thing in "real" life. I wonder if I'll ever make love to Jake like that again. I wonder if he's even still alive. I can't believe I can't contact him, and that it's driving me this crazy. It's not like he asked to come into my dream. It's not like he was consciously even there. I guess I really am having trouble letting go. I want to think this is natural. I'm sure everyone goes through it.*
>
> *What did I learn in this color? I learned that there are more possibilities to time than I had imagined. Maybe it's not so standard, after all. I*

learned that sometimes I don't see things, even when they're right in front of my face, like the possibility of espionage was. I guess I do tend to cling pretty heartily to my little version of reality. I don't like this revelation much, since it means that once in a while Momma or even Jake might be right when I'm sure that they're wrong.

I'm resolving to try to be more open to the possibilities of life. K.

✡ ✡ ✡

June 18

Guide's Journal, Ninth Entry

Karina came very close to being lost in this color. The explosion was forceful. I was lucky that she heard me calling her. I don't know what happened to Jake. I wish there were something I could do to help her.

She learned about the future and the possibility of time travel. I wonder if she will make use of this knowledge. It seemed that she was more concerned about the Earth's energy than her own. I admire her for that, trying to save the world. Still, even with her focusing on this plane of existence, I think she saw that there are a lot more channels to reality than she believed.

I hope she chooses to use this to expand the way she looks at reality. Blessed be.

I've made two laps of the park and still no Jake. He's usually Mr.-On-The-Spot. You can set your clock by his monotonously inflexible routine. I used to admire this in him. Now, of course, it annoys the be-crazies out of me. Except today. Today I need him to be here and he's not. I just hope he's not hurt. Or dead.

I've never done three laps before but I'm going around again. It's been a very long time since I've prayed in the traditional sense, but I decide this is a good time to start. This is another recurring pattern in my life: frustration and despair birth prayer, and not much else. I read once that praise prayer was the best form. Maybe I should learn that.

I come around the bend one last time. Still no Jake. That's it, I'm going home to call him.

I hate the message on his answering machine. "You know how this works. It's a while before the beep."

Where the hell is he, anyway? What do I say: "Are you alive?" I'm not leaving a message. As soon as she sets the phone down, it begins to ring.

"Hello."

"Karina?"

"Jake? I was just trying to call you."

"Yeah, I know. I used that callback function. What's up?"

"Umm. I had a bad dream about you last night, then I didn't see you in the park this morning. Are you all right?"

"Yeah, I had to work a double shift. Someone called in sick and we had a bomb scare. I actually had to detonate the thing. Military training comes in handy."

"Oh, my God."

"What, Karina? What did you dream?"

"That you were blown up."

"Jesus, Karina. What the hell are you doing with that shit? Now you're trying to kill me?"

"I thought you didn't believe in the dreams?"

"I don't. But, you have to admit it's a little weird. The first time in history this city has a bomb, I get called to handle it, and it's the night you dream I get blown up."

"I didn't mean for it to happen. I barely got out myself. If it makes you feel any better, I was trying to save you."

"Thanks for the thought. Do me a favor. In the future just leave me out of your crazy dreams," he says.

My heart is blocking my throat.

"Yeah, sure, I'll leave you out," I whisper.

Chapter Nine - Sky Blue
Probing Problems

Momma is squaring her shoulders. I know there is something unpleasant coming. Ever since I was a young girl I've understood Momma's silent way of initiating confrontation.

"Karina," Momma says, "I know you insist on taking this journey your own way, but I can't stress enough that you must avoid unnecessary danger." Her brow is lowered and her tone is curt

I hate when she addresses me in this way. My rebuttal is sometimes to pull in and retreat, sometimes to advance, causing both of our heads to butt like rams in the field. Today, I just stand my ground.

"I'm not looking for danger, Momma."

"Not looking for it and avoiding it are two different things," she declares.

I take a deep breath, wanting to hold myself intact, to not get all mixed up in Momma's energy this time. "I'll try," I concede. "Didn't you run into any danger when you first took the journey?"

"Sure, I did. But I was careful. All I'm asking is that you be careful."

This is Momma's way of saying that she loves me. I appreciate the thought.

The candles are a soft, light blue. Their flames are burning brightly. After last night, if the only person getting hurt were myself, I'd settle for that, not that I'm asking for trouble.

"Karina," Momma says, "you've been through the tunnel enough to begin understanding it, and you've been in the dream world enough to start to comprehend that all realities are not the same."

Momma never says anything without a purpose. "I'm not sure I like where this is going," I say.

"It's about the tunnel. I told you not to touch it at first, because touching realities we're not ready for can harm us in unspeakable ways."

"What do you mean, 'at first'?" I ask.

"Gradually, you have come to recognize the tunnel, to tune yourself into its energy and intelligence."

"And to be burned by it," I add.

"Technically, yes. But more accurately burned by your own perception of it," Momma says.

"Burned either way," I declare. I am willing to take my chances on the journey, but not to be manipulated into courting injury. "Anyway, didn't you just say I was to avoid danger?"

"Unnecessary danger, Karina. The point I'm trying to make is that you have begun to see the tunnel as more than just a vessel of passage. You felt its regret. You saw its fury and witnessed its imbalance. You heard its heart beat. You sensed its sentience."

Momma pauses. Is it for effect? No. She has passed "the talking stick" to me and I do not know how to respond. I have to speak, because she will sit there, mouth closed, until I do. I learned long ago that no one can outwait Momma in this game. If I agree with her that I've come this far, that I understand the significance of a sentient tunnel, it will be an assent that I'm ready to move on, move further into something I'm still scared of and don't yet comprehend.

"Just because I felt it doesn't mean I understand it," I say.

"Of course you don't fully understand it. Do you understand a new friend the first time you meet, or even the fifth?" she asks.

"That's an unfair question," I say. "You know I don't understand people at all."

"You understand as much as anyone does. You just don't like what you see," she says.

It's true that I don't always like what I see in people. They are confusing and often irrational, but I'm sure there are those who understand better than I do. This, however, is not a point I'm choosing to argue. I play mute.

"Listen to me carefully, Karina. What I'm about to say is important. The trap door, the tunnel, the vessel, it's not what you think it is. It's not what is outside coming at you. It's what is inside you coming out."

"That's preposterous," I say. "You're saying I made a fire and burned myself?"

"Yes," she says.

"Why would I do that?"

"People do it all the time, in various disguises," she says. "Call it a twisted wire in the human psyche, call it a shadow casting itself into the light, it really doesn't matter. People punish themselves in hundreds of little ways every day.

I am stunned by Momma's insight and ashamed to see myself in it. "The tunnel is me?"

"Yes, in these dreams your deepest self congeals into form," she says.

"Then why do I have to be so wary of it?" I ask.

"Because your spirit is very powerful and, at this point, still very uncontrolled. You need to learn to see where the things you create come from and how their energy can absorb you, or how you can choose to absorb their energy."

I look down at the Crystal Goddess so cool on her mat.

What is it about her energy that makes me afraid to be in yet unable to resist it? Her journey is so treacherous to the ego and maybe even to life, but everything seems so much more real - so much more alive - once she has touched it. I may understand more than I think.

"Are you saying that I have to touch the tunnel walls now?" I ask, sure that she can't mean this.

"I'm saying," she says, "that you can touch them when you feel you're ready, however, do so gently; with intention, a pure heart and a good thought in your head."

I look at Momma as though she's a being from another planet. I want to complain that I didn't know the rules were going to change part way through. Hell, I was just learning the first rules. I actually thought I was playing the game quite well until now.

I'm struck by the thought that this journey mirrors my life in too many painful ways.

Momma smiles. "You will be fine," she assures me. "You can begin your journey into this color when you're ready." She closes her eyes and begins to hum.

I don't want to go. I've come to like the feeling of being in the dream world, but I don't like the lack of control I feel coming out of it. I like it even less now, knowing that I am supposed to be the control.

I look at Momma. If I thought she was going to relieve me of this onus, I was wrong. She is still sitting, humming, waiting.

Well, here goes Sky Blue.

"Geiser of reason,
Mother of Truth,
angle my thoughts
through parallels, ruth-

lessly string
their points to a time
when all are connected
each on its own line.

Sending perception
to follow the sky
lead me homeward
when time becomes nigh."

I'm on a bridge, built high over a river. Below, the rushing river has little white caps. The wind is whipping my hair in my eyes. I keep my head down to avoid the sting. A man in an old brown coat and a torn, tasseled hat walks up and stands beside me, blocking my wind. He pulls out a bottle in a paper bag. I'm surprised that the bag is light blue. It looks like an old gift bag. On it is written, "celebrate."

"To your journey," he says, taking a swig.

I take the bottle. "What the heck? To my journey, I say."

I am in the land of clouds. My feet bounce across pillows of air filled with just enough pressure to take my steps and give them back.

The light is special here. Sky blue, the actual color of the crayon I used to stroke across the tops of paper as a child. The light casts everything: the clouds, the air, my skin in varying tones of sky blue.

"Hi." a voice says.

Bouncing around to find it, I see a middle-aged man with blueberry blond hair and a perfectly trimmed beard.

"You're new here, aren't you?" he asks.

"Well, yes, I guess I am."

"Come. I'll show you around."

His bouncing has a rhythm born from years of transporting himself through pounds of air pressure. It looks easier than it is, and he's getting ahead of me.

"Oh, forgive me," he calls, turning to see me in the distance. "I forget that this takes some practice."

We're getting close to a large group of people, all lounging in layers of clouds and laughing.

"This is the community area," he says, as if I would remember how one cloud formation differed from another.

"How do you remember where it is?" I ask.

"Oh, you'll find it easily enough. Just think of it when you want to come here," he says, smiling and winking.

Yeah, right, I think.

"What if you don't want to be with other people?" I ask noticing that there are no structures of any kind.

"Oh, well, then you just make one of these," he says, lifting his hands and sculpting an igloo out of the cloud. "If you think of something you need, you'll probably find you already have it, or can construct it of cloud."

"This is quite a place."

"Yes. It's pretty much perfect, except for that pesky problem with the Earthlings."

"The Earthlings? What pesky problem is that?"

"Oh, those darn satellites they stuck into space. Every time I sit down to meditate, I end up tuned into Al Bundy sitting in front of a television with his hands in his pants; or I see Angela Lansbury snooping around for yet another murderer. Or, if I'm lucky, I catch a much seen episode of

Captain Kirk bumbling about the galaxy in a large metal container, as if that sort of equipment was necessary. This is when I'm not sent into an intolerable depression by the evil reports Earthlings call 'News'. It's most upsetting.

"I have no idea how they stand it. When I go to Earth on my rotation, I have to wear special ear filters. We all do. Otherwise, we wouldn't be able to work effectively. They blither around on Earth like there's nothing wrong. Then, they actually purchase receptor boxes to retrieve the signals. Televisions they call them. Oh, excuse me for babbling on. I guess you already know all of this. You come from Earth, don't you?"

"Well, yeah, but I'd never thought of it quite that way."

"You probably didn't think at all on Earth. How could you? Anyway, I'm sure you couldn't have heard yourself if you did."

"Actually, I can't recall noticing the noise."

"That's what they all say, though I don't understand it."

"Well, if it bothers you that much, why don't you do something about it? Can't you adjust the signals, or block them out."

"We have a policy of non-interference, kind of like your Captain Kirk. Still, we have been forced to try tampering with the equipment. You know, just a little natural breakage. Doesn't work, though. You just fix it. Persistent little buggers, I'll give you that."

He's looking at me like a mischievous child.

"Can you keep a secret? Some of us have tried other things too. We've tried introducing them to non-verbal entertainment. Sent people to stand on street corners to create a resurgence in the fine old art of mime. It didn't really catch on. Funny, we love it here. We've also tried teaching them telepathy. Of course, a few of them can do it by themselves, but we sent experts. Even let them study us in laboratories so they could learn the technique. Nothing. Well, not much."

"There must be something you can do." I say.

"That's why you're here. I was told you were the problem-solver. The Clan is forming a new committee to handle this. Someone will be in touch with you, I'm sure."

"But I don't know anything about satellites. I'm just...journeying. I'm on a search for my inner self."

He laughs a full belly laugh that is very irritating. "Why? Did you lose it?"

"This from a man who thinks Earth people are going to trade Star Trek for mime?" I ask, maybe a bit too sarcastically.

"Well then. I suppose you'll want to be alone to compose yourself. I'll be looking forward to hearing your solution."

He disappeared directly into the clouds. I hope he's wrong. I hope they, whoever they are, don't really expect me to solve their problem. I'm not a Scientist. Well, I may have been one in a dream, but I don't know how that happened. And I certainly don't know anything about satellite frequencies. I'll just tell them so. I'm sure they'll understand.

These clouds are very relaxing to lay on; and there's something extremely soothing in the sky blue light. It is true, though. There is an annoying undercurrent of broadcast pollution. I've tried several different spots and several different positions. So far, I've tuned into a string of medical crises on ER, exciting, but not a very pleasant atmosphere to relax in; experienced tawdry relationship conflicts via Melrose Place; and witnessed an oceanic rescue, courtesy of Bay Watch. I definitely agree there's a problem here.

"There you are. I almost didn't see you under all those clouds. My name is Sarah."

"Hi Sarah. I'm Karina."

"Yes, I know."

"Yeah, I suppose you do."

"The meeting is starting. We were kind of surprised that you hadn't joined us. Didn't you get our communiqué?"

"No, but then..."

"Never mind that. Can you come now?" Sarah is holding her hand out for me to take it.

As I take her hand, we seem to sink into the moistness of cloud pressure. Within seconds we emerge in a cloudroom, where a group of people are convened in a circle. The group shifts as Sarah steps forward and we join the circle.

"Nice wheels." I say. She just looks at me as though I'm speaking a foreign language. "A metaphor for transportation," I explain. "Never mind." I definitely get the feeling that this group thinks they are superior to Earth people, of which I am one. At least I hope I'm still one.

"We're addressing the problem of the satellites," Sarah says to the group. And, then turning to me, "What are your thoughts?"

"Well, I can see they're a problem, but I have no idea what you can do about them."

"Excuse me," says a rather perturbed blue-haired celestial being, "but this is why you are here, isn't it? If I'm not mistaken, and I never am, you are here to solve this problem, and you're not going back until you do. I suggest you think a little harder." Then, turning toward the rest of the group, "we'll reconvene in twenty-four hours."

They all sink slowly into the clouds. I liked the bouncing better.

These people are really obnoxious and downright unfair. I don't care if they do live in a magic space, I have to find a way out of here.

I let out a scream that shakes the clouds. I hope it bursts their sensitive little eardrums. That would solve my problem.

"You called?" In front of me appears a very handsome dark-haired man dressed in a sky blue robe. His eyes perfectly match his garb.

"Jake! What are you doing here?"

"I came because you called. Don't I always come when you call?"

"Well, yes, but how did you get here? How did you find this dimension?"

"We're soul mates. I can follow wherever you go. Actually, I could have come here on my own, except I'd have no reason to do so. But, since you're on this journey, and I'm your partner, I travel when you travel. Hadn't you noticed?"

"But you're not even speaking to me, on Earth."

"Yeah too bad about that - unfortunate turn of events. I've tried to reason with myself, but you know how I am. Once I've been hurt it's hard for me to open up again."

"Is he, the Earth Jake, sleeping? Dreaming so that you can be here?" I ask.

"Oh no. I'm awake there."

"You're in both places at the same time? So why do I have to go to all the trouble of taking this journey, if I could be here without it?"

"For one thing, I won't remember this, at least not consciously. You're building a bridge between the pieces of yourself, consciously. You'll be able to pull them all together in the end, or whenever you need them, assuming you stay conscious of yourself."

"It sounds better than it feels," I say. "If building this bridge is such a great thing, why don't you do it? Why doesn't everyone do it?"

"Oh, lots of people are trying. And some are succeeding. Many would rather not be pulled together. Too much work and too scary. But most just don't know the way."

"What about you? Why don't you, um, get connected?"

"Preoccupied, one. And two, I really thrive on the conflict separation gives me. You know, the exhilaration of a good battle."

"Yeah, I know that."

"Anyway, last I heard there's no rule says you've got to get together in this lifetime."

"Good thing, since I may never have the opportunity if I don't figure out how to solve the celestial noise problem."

"What's the problem?" he asks.

"The problem is the satellites..."

"I heard the story," he says. "But the satellites aren't the problem. What's the real problem?"

"The real problem? The real problem is that these people are tuned into the broadcast frequency and it's disrupting their peace."

"Right. Now, how do they fix that? he asks."

"I don't know how they fix that! What do I look like, Albert Einstein?"

"No. Thank God. You look like the beautiful, smart woman you are."

"Are you sure you're my Jake?"

"The one and only, metaphorically speaking, of course. Karina, I couldn't solve this for you, even if I knew the answer. This is your challenge, but if you look closely enough I know you'll find the solution. That's all I can say."

"The only thing I can think is that it has to be something to do with our brain structure. I've got it! I'll have them analyze me, then they can find the difference between us and them and figure out how to adjust for it."

"There ya go. Good plan."

"Oh Jake. I really miss you. Thanks for being such a great guy." I kiss him long and hard on those luscious lips before I think my way back to Sarah.

Not bad, I came within two bounces. They agree to test me.

We're ten hours into the twenty-four hour time limit and despite all their mental pushing and prodding they've found nothing that distinguishes us from each other. I'm not sure who's more disappointed, them or me.

"Well, you're going to have to think of something else," Sarah says.

"Then you're going to have to let me go back," I say. "The answer is obviously not here."

"It can't be done. Or, it can, but it's dangerous."

"I can't stay here forever, much as I'm enjoying your pleasant company. I'll take my chances."

"You'd have to remain attached to this plane, which means you'd have to go back without a visible image. If you do this, you can't let any Earthlings sense you. Most don't understand the spirit world. They are no problem. But a few are afraid of it and have learned just enough to be dangerous. If they try to exorcise you, you could end up trapped in limbo for...a very long time."

Shit. Jake isn't going to like this. And I was getting along with this one so well.

"I'll take my chances. But I have a stop to make first," I say.

"Go see your friend. When you are ready, just say this rhyme." She hands me a piece of paper. "Say it backwards when you want to come back. And good luck."

I'm having trouble finding Jake. I guess it's because I really don't want to tell him this.

"Looking for me?"

"Hi, handsome. I've got bad news and good news. The bad news is we're the same as them. The good news is they're letting me go back to look for a solution."

"They explained the risk?"

"Yeah, but I can't see any other way. Can you?"

"It's your call, Karina. Do what you have to do. Just be careful. You know I love you."

"I like you much better than the other guy."

"I am the other guy," he says.

"Hard to believe. Are you coming with me?"

"I can't double on the same plane. You can only do this because your consciousness is with you. Mine's already on Earth and, since it's my main dimension, I can't operate there unnoticed by myself. I'd drive myself crazy"

"That sounds pretty confusing. I guess I'll take your word for it."

"Just remember, watch everything that happens very closely," he says.

"Thanks. Here goes everything...

"Out of the swirl
and into the whirl,
swinging through space
not losing my place,
transport me to Earth,
the site of my birth."

It's actually pretty cool being the proverbial "fly on the wall." After being in the Sky Blue dimension, Earth people look different. Most of them look...I don't know exactly what, but it's something...closed, maybe.

I landed in an office building. I've been roaming hallways and eavesdropping on conversations and I still can't seem to quite pin it down. Why don't they hear the noise that the sky people do?

"Do you know what your problem is?" A rather irritated woman says to a man. "Your problem is that you're just plain selfish."

Ouch. It's the old "selfish" argument. Everyone hates that. True or not, it's fighting below the belt. Sensitive area. "Selfish" is the best weapon a mother has because it's indisputable. I despise the "selfish" argument, although I've used it on Jake a few times, with great effectiveness.

This is no use. Time is running out and all I can do is sit here and analyze other people's fights.

"Did you feel that?" A woman at the water cooler asks another."

"Feel what?"

"You're going to think I'm crazy, but I could have sworn I just felt a being pass by."

Oh, shit, she can sense me. How can she sense me when no one else can?

"You've been reading too many auras or something. I still don't understand how you do that," says the woman who didn't sense me.

She's a psychic, or something. I'd better get out of here. Anyway, I don't see any clues. Sarah said that saying the rhyme in reverse would bring me back. So I do it.

Jake is waiting when I arrive. I check his watch. The time went much more quickly on Earth.

"It's been twenty-three and a half hours and I've got nothing. What am I going to do?"

"What did you see on Earth?"

"I saw people doing what they do. Eating, working, arguing. About being selfish. And someone felt me."

"How did she feel you?"

"I don't know. She just seemed to be tuned in where the others weren't."

"Why do you think the others weren't?"

"I'm sure they chose not to."

"But why? Why did they choose not to and she chose to?" Jake asks.

"Well, from my experience, it's easier not to. The world is bent that way."

"The world is bent that way?" he asks, emphatically.

"Yes, the world: the Earth's reality - I mean, the people of Earth's reality. It's, you know, the collective consciousness. Huh! Earth people are smarter than I gave them credit for. Of course, it's "collective consciousness." They're all agreeing together to block out the broadcast, which is creating enough of a force to keep the signals from infiltrating our thoughts.

Why? Wouldn't it have been better to just learn to send our signals telepathically?"

"Not if you wanted to unite an entire planet at an escalated rate."

"The global village thing?" I ask.

"Maybe. It'd be quicker than trying to individually teach each person to connect. It would be easier than urging people to evolve beyond their readiness. Certainly, it would be less costly in terms of mental facilities."

"Do you think that someone, or a small group of people, decided this? Or do you think that we are all in on it, subconsciously?" I ask.

"Let's handle one mystery at a time." Jake says. "At least now you've got an answer to the sky blue problem. Whether these cloud people band together to use it is their decision."

Sarah is looking pale, even for someone standing in the blue light. "Are you implying that Earthlings are more advanced than we are?" she asks.

"No. I'm not saying that we're better or worse; not saying that what we've chosen is good or bad. I'm just saying that we seem to have a different agenda, and we're working our plan toward that end. I've delivered your answer. Do what you want with it. Change your reality or not. I really don't care."

Now, if you'll excuse me, I see my ride." I say this as a beam of clear light flashes through the sky blue background. Sinking into the beam, I slide into a tunnel that looks like dancing stars. I'm aware that it could be hot, but it's so beautiful. Beautiful to look at and powerful to sense. The tunnel feels stronger and less volatile than I remember. Could it be that I'm less volatile? I wonder. Maybe the success of having solved the celestial being's problem has strengthened me.

I slip quickly through this tunnel, as though I'm on a slide. I think of putting my arms out to touch it. Maybe it would slow my ride. Maybe my arms would go right through it. Or maybe it would catch them, break them or burn them. Although Momma said the tunnel is I, I still don't quite trust it. I decide to keep my arms at my sides and just enjoy the show.

I see a bright light and feel the inertia of my slide pulling me back into the world where Momma waits.

Momma looks a little different: less melancholy - maybe, lighter. Yes, lighter.

"What is it, Momma? Why are you so serene?"

"I can't tell you now," Momma says.

"Momma, can you take the journey more than once?"

"You can live in the journey, if you want to," she says. "Most of the time."

"Is that why you always seem so distant? Are you not really here?"

"Karina, it would take me a long time to answer that. But, for right now, all you need to know is that there is only one first journey, and you must take it carefully."

"I'm trying," I say.

"And the tunnel?" she asks.

"The tunnel was a slide, with dancing star walls."

Momma looks at me for a long moment, but says nothing. She puts her hand in mine and we walk to the kitchen feeling a foreign closeness. Gramma is serving a soufflé. Somehow I don't even find it odd that she was able to time this meal so perfectly. Sometimes the universe just fits. I take a deep breath and pull it in, hoping to find many more moments like this.

Dinner was wonderful, but now I feel the need to get out and look at the world. Climbing into my ancient Honda Civic, powder blue and rust, I let out the clutch and shift into reverse. I feel like letting my hair fly in the breeze, so I head for the highway. Cruising a strip of US41, I move the stick into fifth gear and crank the radio up. Bob Seger is singing "Turn the Page."

I don't always check my rear view mirror, so I have no idea how long the lights have been flashing red and blue behind me. I pull over. A police car comes up to my rear. I'm tempted to leave the radio up, but I know how much that irritates the macho squad. I don't recognize the cop who sidles up beside my window, but I think I've seen him before.

"Your license and registration," he says.

I try to smile as I hand it to him.

"You realize you were doing 75 in a 55?"

"No. I guess I was a little distracted."

"Karina Calloway." He says. "Any relation to Jake Calloway?"

"Yes. He's my - actually, no. No relation."

He looks at me with that electric-drill intensity they teach so well at the academy. He's been practicing it for a long time, and he has the wrinkles in his forehead to prove it. I'm sure he knows about Jake and me. The cops in Jake's precinct gossip more than the women in a small-town-sewing-circle. He's probably wondering whether he'd be doing Jake a bigger favor by arresting me or by letting me go.

"Too bad," he says. "Jake's a good man. A good cop. He's a cop's cop, if you know what I mean. That kind of man can be hard to live with, at least that's what my ex-wife always said. Anyway, I sure hope he finds a woman who will treat him the way he deserves. You can go now, Karina. Just don't let me catch you speeding again. You're not immune to the law anymore."

Jesus, what a bastard! I'd like to take that badge and use it to puncture a few well-placed nerves. "I hope he finds a woman...you're not immune." I can't believe the mentality of this public servant. They should have to pass some sort of socio-psychological adjustment test before they're allowed to roam the streets.

Take it easy, Karina. I remind myself. You know his type. That's why his wife dumped him. That's why all their wives dump them. That's why you divorced Jake. But Jake's not as bad as this guy is. Still, if nothing changes, in twenty years - there goes Jake.

I drive toward a nearby town. Cars pass me, since I am now going the speed limit. That cop hit a cord in me with his assessment of Jake and his judgment of me. That a man like him, someone who thinks in only one unvarying line, could decide that I am not worthy of Jake annoys me. Relationships are the most difficult thing about life. How could he understand that I feel like I lose my sense of power whenever I give into Jake's way of controlling our relationship. I hate control issues. I try to control my own anger as I make my way home.

I'm glad to be settled into my room where, hopefully, no one will barge in and start telling me how to live my life. I suppose I should write in my journal before I go to sleep.

✛ ✛ ✛

June 19

Tenth Journal Entry: Sky Blue

In Sky Blue, I learned that human weakness is also a form of strength. Our seeming inability to communicate sensorially was actually born of a need to connect with people who were not ready to do so, emotionally. We overrode our natural evolution and escalated the process through technology. On a large scale, humans cover our unwillingness to get close to one another with a mass communications system that will keep us in touch, without the touch. I'm beginning to believe the old saying that "everything happens for a reason."

I discovered that I have to give humankind credit for joining together despite a formidable group-fear against doing so. Many people have been removed from their comfort zone just by the idea of new media options.

In Sky Blue, my personal comfort zone was challenged. The celestial beings acted superior to me and I let them have that power. At first, my inferiority made me feel inadequate to the task they gave me. Then, I became angry. I felt I had to prove my worth by going back to Earth, even though it was a risk to my very existence. My ego was in possession of my emotions. Next, I felt that old "control urge" take over. I felt I could be of some value if I could just fix their problem. Wanting to take back the power, I let their problem become my problem. Luckily, I finally realized that I am not responsible for their situation, nor am I responsible for their reactions to my choices. I am responsible only for being true to what is inside me.

The Jake I met in Sky Blue was kind. He gave me the space to make my own decisions, to be true to myself. He actually supported my decisions. And the weirdest part was, he was the same Jake that gives me no space on Earth. Could it be that there's more to him than I am currently seeing? Like the cloud people, It may be that I am trying to solve a problem for him. I hope I remember to listen to what's inside me in coming to terms with Jake. K.

June 19

Guide's Journal, Tenth Entry

Karina learned a valuable lesson about the power of the subconscious today, and one about the strength of human beings. She's a smart girl. The assignment they gave her was not an easy one. I didn't like her traveling back and forth between worlds, with so little experience. Still, it was her choice and she did well.

I wonder if she understood what Jake told her about the subconscious traveling without our awareness and the consciousness traveling with it. It's not so different, really, from how we operate on the Earth plane. Even that takes a little mental gymnastics to understand. It's much easier just to be quiet and listen to one's inner voice. Karina seems to prefer the mental gymnastics at this stage. I just hope the lessons of control and inner-listening stick with her. It will help her put everything together later.

I'm glad the Jake she met was really nice. They've all been nice, which makes me wonder whether she just does not understand her Earth Jake. Makes me wonder whether she is willing her dream "Jakes" to be nice so that she can like them, or whether she is soon going to run into a Jake with the qualities she claims to really despise. Blessed be.

Chapter Ten - Dark Blue
Defining Destiny

Momma has gone to some extra lengths for this color. For the first time, she has music playing in the background, soft flute music. She is humming in time with it. There is a navy blue, crocheted doily under each candle, and a larger one under the Goddess. She allowed me longer in my bath than usual, a luxury I cherish. The frankincense and flower essences have settled into my being like the spirits of my ancestors. They hug warmly around me without smothering my own essence.

Momma rubs my shoulders. "She'll be with you," she says.

"She?" I ask.

"The Goddess," Momma says, nodding to the austere statue who holds millenniums of wisdom compressed into one piece of finely formed glass.

"I thought that was the point," I say, "of the whole journey."

"Yes, but this is different. You'll see."

"Aren't you going to tell me more about the tunnel?" I ask.

"I will tell you when you need to know it."

She begins chanting and swaying back and forth. There is a smile on her face. She seems to really like this color, and I'm curious to know why.

I begin my rhyme to dark blue.

"Spinner of destiny,
worker of webs,
capturing moments:
energy's ebbs.

Rainbow Goddess: A Journey Tale

*Giver of wisdom
discernment and pride,
hide not your gifts
in turbulent tides
of space and time
and emotional rifts.
Teach me to follow
correctional shifts.*"

I'm in the lobby of an exquisite hotel. The furniture is upholstered in deep navy blue, accented with heavily fringed gold ottomans. The bases of the lamps are crystal and brass, and the shades are blue velveteen. The look is executive and rich. A man dressed in a black tuxedo with a navy blue bow tie is walking toward me.

"Ms. Calloway, I presume?"

"Yes."

"If you will kindly follow me," he says. Then he turns on his heels. The shoes, I notice, have a perfectly polished shine. I follow him into the lounge and over to a table where a woman is waiting.

"Your guest has arrived," he announces, bows slightly, and turns to leave.

"Won't you have a seat?" she asks. She twirls her wrist gracefully, offering me the only other chair at the table.

"Thank you." I sit and wait for her to speak, but she doesn't. She just smiles and looks into my eyes.

After what seems like ten minutes, but is probably closer to one, a waiter comes with two glasses of blue liquor.

She slowly lifts her glass. "To your journey," she says.

I lift my glass and hope that my journey will be as gentle and elegant as she.

I'm in a hole in the frame of space. Stars glitter large and light around me. In front of me a woman sits on a throne. She is glowing. An angel-like being is sitting in a chair to her left, and many other beings are above and behind her. There is an empty chair to her right.

"Come. Sit beside me," she says, looking at me. She looks like every picture I have ever seen of the Virgin Mary, Aphrodite and the Earth Mother all woven together.

As I take my seat, a group of young girls dance their way onto the space in front of us. They are performing some type of ballet. Some of them are very young. One is maybe three. Her routine consists mostly of pliets and pirouettes. This makes me smile. One has perfect form. Her muscles do whatever she tells them to, right on time. One is obviously new to this, but is trying very hard to follow the group. They are all lovely to watch. When the dance ends, everyone applauds.

"Which touched you most?" Mary asks.

"How can I choose? They were all so wonderful."

"I know, but which reached into your heart the deepest?"

"Do I have to choose one?"

"Choosing is part of responsibility. If you want to know how this color works, you will have to learn to make decisions. I ask again, which touched you most?"

"I guess it would be the littlest one. Dancing those same steps over and over," I say.

She is nodding her head, as if in agreement, but to what I'm not sure. The dancers have gone as quickly as they came. I'm sorry to see them go.

One of the angel-beings is holding a large glass ball and bringing it close to us so we can look into it.

"It is a message for you," Mary says.

I look into the ball and see the trees and the grass in the park where I jog. Anne Calloway is there, jogging alone. A man is running up behind her. He's reaching his arm around her and pulling her off into the trees. Anne is struggling. She kicks, and then bites him. But he's too strong for her. He is trying to get himself inside her.

"Can't we do something?" I ask Mary.

"We are doing something." She says. "Just watch. You will see."

Anne's clothes are torn. The man is getting very close to his goal. Bob, the salesman I had a premonition of seeing her with, comes running along the path. He hears her cries and goes to see what's happening. He gives the attacker a karate-style sidekick to the head and another to the chest. When he reaches down to pull Anne away, the attacker runs off. As the attacker disappears into the bushes Jake comes on the scene. He takes one look at Anne and punches Bob in the face so hard that it knocks him over.

"That's the guy who was hitting on Karina," Jake says.

"No." Anne says. "Not him." She is sobbing.

"What do you mean not him?"

"It wasn't him," Anne says.

"Who then?"

"Ran away," she says.

"Which way?"

"Through those trees," Bob says, pulling himself up.

"Will you be all right?" Jake asks Anne.

"Yeah." Anne nods. Jake runs off, not even bothering to apologize to Bob.

I see Bob comforting Anne. I'm amazed that he was there to help her, but not as amazed as I would have been before I traveled through sky blue. My new motto is "everything happens for a reason."

"Should I go see her?" I ask Mary.

"Not now." Mary says. "She'll be all right. Bob will take care of her."

"Do you see everything that happens from here?"

"Some we see. Some we feel. One way or another we keep track of everything."

"Can I see more?"

"Look into the glass," she says.

"Who is that girl?" I ask.

"That is my friend, Shannon."

"Why does she have so many angels around her?"

"She does my work, and that is unpopular with some of the people there. She needs special protection."

The picture has shifted to a woman in an expensive blue suit, carrying a briefcase.

"Why doesn't she have any angels?" I ask.

"She refuses them. Absolutely closes her mind to outside help. Pity too. Her life is being wasted and she doesn't even realize it."

The picture changes again. It's like watching a movie with the camera panning far into the distance. I can see the whole planet.

"What are those lights? They look like they form some sort of grid."

"You're right. Whenever thoughts or action occur within each of the squares, the energy of the grid absorbs and processes it, creating the appropriate reaction. Some call them karmic zones."

"I always wondered how that worked. I have to admit, I thought it was a little more ethereal," I say.

"Karmic energy can be as ethereal or non-ethereal as you want to make it. The point is, it lives and reacts with other energy vibrations. I can interrupt it with my thoughts from here, but only do so occasionally. Most times, it's amazingly self-correcting," Mary says.

"So, it's true that the state my life's in is entirely my choice?" I ask rather weakly.

She doesn't answer. Just looks at me as if I know better than to ask. I didn't really mean it as a question any way. More an admission of a guilt I've always known was there.

"Can I look more closely, see how it works?" I ask.

"You have gone to a great deal of effort to be here, so I am going to give you a very special tour."

As she says this, the stars that were lighting the sky begin to dim, or recede, and the blue around me becomes deeper and stiller, until I am in a very dark space. Then, without warning, I am transported back to Earth.

I'm sitting in my car, stopped at a red light. I look around. I'm alone. I look down at the seat and notice a folder. Inside the folder are the divorce papers I filed to dissolve my marriage to Jake. Looking closer, I notice that they're unsigned. For the briefest of seconds I am relieved. Under the folder is a newspaper. It's old. It's from the date I filed for divorce. Am I going to relive that whole horrible ordeal? Goddess, I hope not.

"Goddess? Mary?" I call out. "I hope this is a guided tour."

"Self-guided," says a very soft voice. And then there is silence.

"Shit. I hate this."

A horn is beeping insistently from behind. "Oh, hold your horses." I say.

I must be on my way to the lawyer's office. Should I keep going? Does this mean that I have the option to change my mind, or am I playing out a karmic reaction to all the ways I've already let this relationship die?

The man behind me obviously thinks I'm driving too slowly. If we were any closer we'd be attached. If I'm not going to the lawyer, then I should turn at the next corner. The light is red. Good. A couple more minutes before I have to decide.

He really isn't a bad guy. I mean, I do still love him.

"He's oppressive and he's dragging you down." A voice inside my head says.

No.

"Yes."

Well, okay, yes. But he doesn't mean to.

"Do you want to live like this, depressed, angry and unappreciated for the rest of your life?"

No, of course not. But, parts of him are really nice. And sexy. I'm going to get lonely, very lonely..

"Better lonely than insane."

Shit, I'm already insane. Listen to me. I can't even think without arguing with myself.

"Honk. Honk. Honk, honk, honk, honk."

"Either get Valium or get laid, Buddy." I say. Indecision really puts me in a foul mood.

I'm passing the intersection and can't seem to stop myself from going straight. I find a parking spot a few buildings down on the right. It's the same one I used last time. I guess nothing has changed. Except the honker in that car behind me. He wasn't here last time. So, maybe my hesitation - my thoughts - have changed something in the karmic response, but not enough.

I take some time to look through the folder. It all seems pretty cold and sterile. A language made perfunctory and technical. Pretty imperfect for severing a bond that was secured by emotion. I'll never understand these things.

I pick up the folder and get out of the car. As I walk toward the door I know that once I enter the lawyer's office it'll all be over. Attorney Leibowitz has a way of making me feel that I'm doing the right thing, that I'd be a fool to do anything else. Whenever I'm hesitant, he reminds me of things I've said about Jake.

"He makes you feel inadequate," he repeats to me. "You feel disempowered when you're with him. He doesn't see you as an intelligent person, capable of making your own decisions."

I open the door.

"Hi, Ms. Calloway," his secretary says. They always use the term "Ms." I suppose they don't want to remind you that you are giving up the title "Mrs." with all the attachments that society gives to that.

"I know you have a two o'clock appointment with Attorney Leibowitz, but he was just called away on an emergency. His brother had a heart attack while driving down the street, just a few blocks over. If you have all the paperwork we sent you, I can have another Partner help you with this."

"Another Partner? I haven't met any other Partner."

"Oh. If you would rather wait for Attorney Leibowitz, I can reschedule you for tomorrow. I'm very sorry."

She doesn't even try to sound sorry. Like this is just another legal spat. A settlement made, a few lives shifted around, it's all the same to her. Ho hum. Well, fuck that.

"I'll call you when I have time," I say. Then I turn and leave.

Back in my car it sinks in that I didn't file for the divorce. Will I do it tomorrow? I don't know. Probably. Maybe. Leibowitz was called away on an emergency.

Unbelievable.

"No, very believable, if you were paying attention."

"Who said that? Mary?"

"You can come back now."

Like walking into a movie theater, light turns to dark in a matter of seconds, and I am transported back into the heavens.

"It felt so real." I say to Mary.

"It was real."

"Do you mean that I'm not divorced from Jake? But, what about all the time that's gone by since the divorce? What happens to that?"

She gives me a quiet little laugh. "Calm down. Every action that happens is not written in stone. What happened then is real, and what happened now is real. When you live on Earth you get so used to the world of form that you forget there is more than one reality. I'm going to send you back now. Just try to remember what happened here, pay attention to what happens there, and learn from it all."

The sky darkens again, and then turns to light. I squint my eyes to see that I am in a narrow tube. Light is shining brightly into my eyes. I step forward into a place in the shadow of the wall. Shielded from the light now, I look down the tube. It has to be the tunnel. But it doesn't seem to be whole. I focus on the spaces where the light is brightest and see that there is nothing to separate the inside from the out. The tunnel has big, oddly shaped holes. I want to look through them, but the light is so bright it is blinding.

Momma said the wall is "I," a part of me, and that I can touch it when I'm ready. If this is I, why do I have big holes? And what is on the other side of those holes? I could reach my arm through, or maybe just the tip of my finger.

I walk out of the shadow and into the next light. Looking at the misshapen window, my eyes nearly closed in an attempt at protection, I try to force myself to touch it. My arm won't move. My eyes fully closed now, I begin to sense a powerful energy flowing in from the opening. I don't need to touch it to know that it is stronger than I am. A shiver of fear runs through my nerves.

When I open my eyes, the hole is gone. As I walk through the tunnel, all the holes in front of me close. I'm beginning to feel claustrophobic. Like I'm in a house on a very hot day and someone is slamming every window shut. But there is no glass. They are all made of wall.

Will I ever get out of here? What about the light that is supposed to be my exit?

I begin to run down the tunnel. It's so dark. My heart is pounding through my chest. The walls seem to be pulsing in time with my heart. My feet feel like they're tripping underneath me, but momentum is carrying me forward.

"Breath, Karina Breath," I tell myself, panting from exhaustion.

I try to keep a straight line, and I run. The space in front of me is developing shadows. Everything is blurry, but there must be light. I keep running, until the ground runs out from under me. I am in a free fall. I close my eyes.

When I focus my eyes, I see Momma. At first glance, I think that she bears an uncanny resemblance to Mary.

"Momma?"

"Yes, Karina. I'm here."

"What day is it?"

"It's the same day you left."

Momma never lies, but still I doubt that this is entirely true.

"You seem a little frightened," Momma says.

"It was the tunnel," I say. "It opened and then closed. I mean parts of it did. The openings were so strong, so powerful. And then they closed. It was dark, and closed."

"Karina, you have only a few more days of travel. You are going to have to master the tunnel. You can't complete the journey unless you do," Momma says. "Come, let's get dinner."

Gramma made a soup made of butternut and acorn squash. She serves it topped with chopped green onions, pine nuts and tortilla chips. The flavors are so dense that I think I can taste the Earth growing up inside the squash, the trees and the tall stalks of corn. It's really good to be back in this dimension. I used to think that life here was hard, but not anymore. True, it does have an edge, but it also has substance: warm, tangible, teddy bear substance.

"Karina looks good." Gramma says.

"Yes, she does." Auntie Connie always agrees with Gramma. Of course, this could be because Gramma is always right, or because she only shares what she knows is right.

"Karina, we are going to be performing a celebration of The Summer Solstice tonight. Would you like to join us?" Gramma asks.

I've never joined in their rituals before. The truth is I've always been a little afraid of them. But tonight I feel honored at the invitation.

"I suppose I could try it."

"There is nothing to try, Karina. You just do what feels right to you: Sing, dance or watch. Just your being with us will be a nice lift to the energy of the group," Gramma says.

Gramma's never said anything about my energy before, and I'm a little embarrassed at the eagerness this compliment makes me feel. I have to control myself to keep from looking like a puppy being praised by her master for fetching a paper.

We do a ritual cleansing and anoint ourselves with oils. There are separate oils for each of the chakras. We visualize the color of the chakra as we anoint. Red for the first chakra at the base of the spine; then orange for the area below the belly button; yellow for the solar plexus, above the belly; green for the heart; turquoise at the throat; indigo for the third eye; amethyst on the crown.

Gramma asperges a ceremonial circle with water and salt, cleansing the area of negative influences. Together we place candles around the circle, stopping to alert the quarters: earth, air, fire and water. We call to the North, South, East and West for guidance and protection, to preserve and guard the power we will raise. We stand around the circle, our feet on the line.

"The circle is to remind us," Gramma says, "that we always stand on the edge of the Visible and Invisible worlds, and that their connection is inseparable. From this circle our energy lifts and concentrates until it forms a cone of power, like a pyramid, which protects us and intensifies our work. Tonight we gather to praise the Goddess and the God and to thank them for the gifts of light and darkness on this, the longest day of the year."

Then Gramma begins to chant a verse. Momma and Auntie Connie join in.

"Light beget shadows,
Shadows give form
to all which come in
and go out again.

Cycle unbroken
lend all forms a home
to shine when they're brightest
to lay when they rest."

For the good of all,
an it harm none.

We hold hands and dance, swaying around the circle. I feel the power of the earth begin to rise up through my soles. It ascends my body, filling me like smoke from a fire rising through air. I am one with the ground, the air and the moon. I am all forms of life, merging at once. I am all the women of the circle joined together in ritual and in blood.

Music floats from flowers and trees, from Gramma and Momma and Auntie Connie. The beauty of their voices and the vision of the thought it holds mesmerize me. Tonight I am honored to be a part of this Wiccan family. Tonight, I am whole.

Fears melt from me as my ego drifts into nothingness.

I've always been afraid of death, thinking that I would go somewhere far, far away. Now it feels that when I'm dead, I'll be very close by, if not on "top" of where I am here. Like, I'll be the frosting instead of the cake. In another layer, but still very yummy.

Knowledge of the whole is mysterious, but scary as I once feared.

I know that the journey has brought me to this. The lessons of the colors, the people I've met have changed me. Mary was so comforting. Everything seemed so right, so orderly in blue, her color. After spending time with the Goddess, I can't help feeling that eventually everything will work itself out.

After the celebration, I lie in my bed feeling too awake and alive to sleep. I have a shoe box full of photographs that I haven't looked at in a really long time. I take some out, and the first four I see are pictures of Jake.

Oh Jake, I wish I could share tonight with you. Explain to you what I felt. What I did. What I didn't do. What I feel now. What would I say to you? Would I tell you what I see in these pictures?

Would I say, "In this one you are looking straight into the eye of the camera, daring it to capture the tiniest part of your essence. Threatening it with a silence that I can still hear, as loud as thunder and twice as frightening.

"In this one you are passionate about whatever it was you were sure of just then. Your eyebrows are raised, your Adam's apple bulging and your hands held in a defiant fist, clenched large and looming. Your friend, Jimmy, is standing next to you, nodding, believing that you are right, as always.

"In this one you are brooding, head hung slightly for effect, like a school boy caught in something he shouldn't have done, but sure that it would have been okay if only I hadn't been there to see your foolishness and label it that.

"In this one. This one I don't remember. In this one you are happy. Smiling into the searching eye, accepting for a change the camera is there in your face. That it wants you. Wants to capture and keep you in a slice of time. And maybe you are even giving it a chance to be your friend. Funny that I don't remember this one. I really like it."

I know there is unfinished business in my heart with Jake. I just don't know how you "finish" love.

❖ ❖ ❖

June 20

Eleventh Journal Entry: Dark Blue

I came back to the Earth, to my life, in this dream. I don't know how real it was, but it surely felt real. I met the Virgin Mother Mary, and she was so kind. And so beautiful, beautiful in a way that goes far beyond the physical. If nothing else had happened, her brightness and love would have been a lesson in itself, but I know she was trying to tell me more.

She made me choose a dancer, and I don't know why. Maybe just to show that I could make a choice. Maybe to show me that I had made a choice, whether or not I realized it. That being conscious of the choice was important. She showed me a vision of Earth events in a crystal ball. They unfolded according to a pattern that even the angels felt and responded to. I'll never again think that I am completely alone, or that my actions don't have reactions.

I'm sure I should understand more of this dream, for example: Why I didn't file for the divorce? I felt like something in me was different, that I wasn't who I had been. Somehow that changed everything. Changes within me change my environment, that much I understand. But there's more than that. The grid was so complex. Each change on it affected everything else. Also, there seemed to be infinite

possibilities for points of change. I'll definitely have to pay more attention to my choices in the future.
Mary sure was beautiful. K.

June 20

Guide's Journal, Eleventh Entry

Karina had a very special journey. She had a chance to change her past and did. The Goddess showed her the workings of karma in a very literal way. I'm not sure that Karina understands what happened yet. She seems a little out of touch, almost like she's emotionally dazed.

Of course, everyone becomes dizzy with love when they meet The Goddess for the first time. But Karina seems to be affected more than most. Maybe I'm wrong. Maybe it was just the Summer Solstice celebration, the way she let herself go and dance with the wind.

On a concrete note, she didn't file the divorce papers, and there will be ramifications to that. Blessed be.

Chapter Eleven - Purple
Spirits Soar

In spite of the strangeness of my dark blue dream last night, nothing seems to have changed in my life. I woke up in my own bed this morning, in Momma's house. I went downstairs and checked the basement, and all my stuff is there. I'm skipping my jog in the park, just in case that part was real. I know I should call Anne, but I'm afraid to.

"Momma, can we start the journey early today?" I ask.

"Sure, Karina, but why?"

"I just...want to."

Momma looks at me closely. "I'll run the water," is all she says.

The water feels like a blanket of warm silk. I breathe in the roses and breathe out my cares. I find it hard to believe that in the natural selection process humans chose land over the ocean. The dolphins really were the smart ones. I close my eyes and watch my breath ride in and out of me like waves, surging and retreating.

"The room is ready, Karina," Momma calls.

"Just one more minute, please, Momma," I say.

I stumble a little as I step out of the tub. The water was pretty hot, and I'm kind of heady from deep breathing the incense. The feeling of being off-balance reminds me of the tunnel I was in last night. Momma comes in with the robe.

"Are you all right?" she asks.

"Fine."

She wraps the robe around me and we go to join the Crystal Goddess. The candles are deep purple. There are fresh violets in a vase. The room looks inviting.

"I want you to pay special attention to the tunnel this time," Momma says. "I want you to become one with it."

"Why?"

"It's very important that you reach out beyond the confines of your body self. You've had plenty of time and experience with it by now. It's very important that you know how far your energy extends, and owning the tunnel is a good first step."

"What if I never touch the wall?" What if I never learn to control it?" I ask.

"Then you won't complete the journey," Momma says.

The tone of her voice is low, cold and somehow threatening. I get the impression that this is not a good option.

Momma turns her head and closes her eyes. She sits beside me and begins to hum a couple bars.

I begin my rhyme.

"Lasoo-er of visions
throw your rope 'round
the clouds and the roots
dug deep in the ground.

Pure energy calmed
by essence of love,
reach into your depth
below and above.

Steal from your canyons
the echoes on high.
Gather your birds
that heaven might fly.

Lend me a caldron

> *to gather your light.*
> *When twilight fades*
> *I'll sprinkle the night."*

I'm in a place where the vines grow high and big balls of purple hang from their foliage, like little planets clumped together in their own private solar system. That there are thousands of these little leafy worlds growing right next to each other is amazing to me.

"I agree. They're spectacular," says a tall, handsome man with high cheekbones and an attractively strong nose. His eyes are penetrating under thick, bushy brows.

"I'm sorry. Allow me to introduce myself. Demetrious, at your service." He bows slightly as he says this.

"Hi, Demetrious. I'm Karina."

"Yes, Karina. It's a lovely name for a lovely woman. These grapes are some of my best. Would you like to sample them?"

"Yes, please. They look delectable." I say.

Demetrious walks over to a bottle and uncorks the top.

"The secret to life and the secret to good wine are the same. Knowing when to let the process rest and when to drink it up is the key to enjoying both. Don't you think?"

"It sounds like a good philosophy to me," I say.

"To the journey of a beautiful woman, then," he says. We clink our glasses and drink together.

I am in a field of sparking crystal. The only plant life is a towering tree with the purple leaves of autumn covering my head like a hole-filled umbrella. Looking through its branches, I am stunned by the beauty of a violet sun. It is setting between two large breasts of mountain pushing into the sky. A cast of purple rays falls from the sun onto the crystal below.

Ahead there are stones, large and round, tall and angular, laid in a pattern I don't understand. Walking toward the stones, I begin to feel their energy. It's strong. Maybe they are another Stone Hedge. I've heard there are many rock settings aligning the Earth's energy paths.

"Hi, Karina," I turn to see my travelling companion.

"Jake, I didn't see you there. I'm glad you're here."

"Me too," Jake says. "I like it when we meet this way."

"Do you know about this color?" I ask. "There's something eerie about the strength of this much beauty all in one place." I've come to think that Jake knows more that he tells.

He looks at me skeptically. "It's the color of re-alignment. But then, you know that."

I know no such thing. How do I tell him that what he said isn't true without calling him a liar? His face looks handsome, and gentle. His blue eyes are filled with sparkle. I really don't want to offend him.

He laughs a bubbling chuckle. "You won't offend me," he says.

"You can read my thoughts?" I ask, more than a little embarrassed.

"You can read mine too, if you'd stop chattering with yourself long enough to listen. But don't stop on my account. It's lovely. Really."

"Glad I amuse you."

"Now look who's offended," he says, still laughing.

"If you weren't so cute I'd stay mad," I say.

"Good. You got that out of your system. Now, let's get started. I'm glad to see you wore hiking boots."

I look down at my attire. I'm wearing the boots, a T-shirt and some sort of purple painter's pants, with a bazillion pockets in them. The pockets are filled with gadgets. I start digging in them for a quick inventory, hoping for clues of what this trip will hold. There are tissues, some string, and an oversized Swiss army knife with a corkscrew. Everything a girl needs, sans the bottle of wine.

Jake turns and starts on a path that only he can see. Criss-crossing between stones and doubling back without apparent reason. I follow.

"Can I ask where we're going?"

"We're following your directions," he says, continuing to walk.

"But I'm not saying, or even thinking any directions. For that matter, I don't even know where I am."

"There are many levels to communication. And you do know this place, Karina. You've been here many times, following this path."

I look up at the mountain breasts. A thought pops into my head. "It's the dance that opens the mountains," I say. Not knowing how or why I know that.

Jake winks at me and places a large, careful hand on my shoulder. He gives me a soft squeeze and my body remembers him. We've been here before. Done this. Felt this before. I begin to walk and he follows me. As we complete the dance, a path begins to light in front of us. The stones glow in a trail that leads to an opening in the rock, which I wouldn't have seen otherwise.

We follow the path and slip into a crystal forest. Quartz stones are growing in all sizes and intensities, some a soft amethyst, others a deep, royal purple. The sun catches at almost every angle. Jake holds my arm, motioning me to be silent and still. Following his gaze, I see a Bengal tiger sauntering agile across and between crystal peaks.

"We'll have to be really careful not to catch his attention," he says.

"Count me in," I whisper.

After what seems a decent amount of time, we move again, heading in the direction of the tiger's path. Hoping he is long and far down the road.

"Exactly where are we going?" I ask.

"To the source."

"Right. What source? And where is it?"

He's looking at me like I'm a two-year old child, and he the patient adult, trying to remain calm. I watch his chest heave in and out as he takes a few deep breaths.

"Karina, you have to get with me on this. You know the way. We've been over this before."

"Between the breast? Is that where we're going. Come on, Jake, help me out. I'm having trouble pulling this back. I'm distracted. There's something in the starkness that seems to call to me, but it feels so far away."

"Then listen," he says. He eyes me carefully, judging something that I'm not sure I want to know about. "Yes, between the breasts."

He steps in front of me and holds my hand. We're climbing down a jagged crystal staircase. The steps are uneven and he is bracing his arm to lend me support.

"Shhh," he says, stopping us. "No. It was nothing."

He leads me to the bottom of the steps. The trail begins to incline again. I can't help watching the way he moves. Stepping softly, carefully, while balancing the weight of a muscular body and well-sculpted, wide shoulders. He leans into each step and sways the rest of his body in perfect balance. Still holding hands, I feel like we're dancing some elaborately choreographed number. I feel that this brilliant setting is the ballroom and someone has forgotten the music.

Lulled by my thoughts, I don't notice the muscles on his neck and arm tightening, his hand slipping from mine, until the tiger is nearly on him. Jumping from behind a deep purple cluster of overgrown crystal, stretched to a length of almost ten feet, the tiger has the advantage of surprise.

"Jake," I shout. "Here. Here."

He breaks his concentration and looks to me in time to see that I'm throwing a knife. The blade draws the reflecting light from the forest of bouncing reflections. It glimmers like a blinding bolt of lightening, flying through the sky. The tiger sees it and is stopped. His eyes stick on the blade. He should run, but is mesmerized into his death as the blade finds and pierces a spot in the middle of his head.

"Dear Goddess, I'm sorry," I say.

"You're as white as sugar." Jake says.

"I didn't mean to kill him."

"You had to. He would have killed me. It's all right." He takes my hand again and kisses it. "I, for one, am happy with your choice."

I look into his pools of blue and think that I could dive way down into his soul.

"I've missed you, Karina," he says.

"I've missed you too, Jake."

He leans close enough to smell my skin, then lets his lips find mine. We begin to drink, softly, the essence of each other, wetting our appetites for more. First nibbling, then devouring like hungry animals in desperate need of the full-belly meal the other can provide. We feed.

Without thought for the other wild life, we abandon our caution. Laying on a fallen crystal, the smooth chill against my back and then his, balancing the heat of the other side. Grasping and passing the feast until we are filled beyond nourishment, until we have tasted the delicacy of desert and said, "Ahh."

We lay for a while watching clouds float across the purple sky.

"A nice cup of cinnamon coffee, that's what I want," I say.

"Then that's what you'll have, when we finish our journey," he says.

"Oh, that. The energy in that spot had better be as good as I remember it, if I have to get up from you to reach it."

"You remember?"

"Yeah. Amazing how a little - okay a lot - of good sex will clear your head."

He smiles and offers me his hand. I accept. We gather our clothes and move on.

Not far ahead is the base of the mountain. The pass between the peaks is high, with scads of protruding sharp edges.

I don't remember having to scale that thing." I say.

"What do you remember?"

"I remember darkness and cold and then warmth and light. A tunnel. There is a tunnel somewhere."

Closing my eyes, I see the outline of a door. It's underneath a piece of crystal overhang.

"It's there," I say. And we walk toward the entrance. There's a small, clear handle on the door. It slides easily when I touch it.

"Tiger-slaying ladies first." Jake says.

I step into the deep chill of the dark purple quartz. The path is smooth and we move quickly, holding in our minds the promise of warmth on the other side.

After a bone-chilling hike through the darkness, we see trickles of light and feel waves of heat rolling toward us.

"Someone is home," he says. "And the furnace is on."

Passing through the arch of the tunnel, we stand in silent awe. We are in the base of a shining crystal bowl. It's so filled with peace and raw, vibrating energy that I'm sure this must be where God and Goddess come to dance, leaving the flow of their movement and the ring of their music to echo against the gleaming walls; to bow and to curtsy, to spin and to dip endlessly, endlessly on in time.

I feel my molecules begin to shift. Breathing deeply, my skin tingling with the vibrations of love skittering through the air, I look at Jake and see that he is shining like a god.

"This," I say, "Is afterglow."

The wind begins to whirl around me. I am wrapped in a funnel of energy. I close my eyes as it lifts me up. I let it pull me into itself. The whirl has a friendly feel to it. It is covering me like a cocoon, a blanket that I want to curl up into and fall asleep forever. Then I remember Momma's admonishment. "You won't complete the journey." And I wonder if that's okay. If I can ever go back to the life I had before my color travels, knowing that this whole other world, worlds are out there. Can I ever be happy just waking and sleeping and moving quietly through my days again?

No. Slumbering through my life is not going to be good enough, anymore. Which means, I am going to have to touch the wall.

I silently curse Momma. She has always done this to me. Pushed me beyond the point of no return.

I force myself to focus on the wall. It is a mass of tongues of purple and yellow fire, licking, laughing, and longing for me. I hear the quiet chuckles inside the tunnel walls. Is this what I thought felt friendly? It's a warm laugh, not menacing, but it's constant. Now that I hear it clearly, I feel like I know that laugh well. Like an ambient noise one learns to tune out, but which, nevertheless, is always there. I feel its' longing for me to join it, to take my place inside its cells, inside the DNA that gives it form. My DNA? I feel it licking at me, extending itself for a taste of what external secrets I might hold. I feel it wanting to partake of the knowledge stored in my field of energy, wanting to connect to it. Digest it. Synthesize it.

Fear sets in. If I go to it, will it open itself and swallow me whole? Will I become it? And if I do, will I ever recognize myself as a self again? Is this the end of me?

I begin to shrink from the wall, kicking and struggling to keep myself away from its leering, groping edges.

"Stay where you are," I shout. "Leave me alone."

The wall obeys. The tongues slide back into a solid mass and go about the business of becoming a wall again.

I look for the light. I see a spark and go frantically toward it. Finding the hole, I jump through with all my strength.

I open my eyes to see Momma smiling, her face shining like Jake's in the bowl.

I am reminded that she is taking this journey with me. I'd like to ask her how she's doing it, but I know what she will say: "Concentrate on your own journey now, Karina. We will talk about the rest later."

And she is probably right. I do have a lot to think about now. I still don't understand how Jake can be so wonderful in my dreams and so difficult here. It's like he's two different people. One on the inside, and one with something extra on the outside. Something that repels me and rejects me.

"Momma, can someone be two people at the same time?" I ask.

"Someone can be lots of people at the same time, if they can handle it. Most people have trouble being one."

Well, there you have it. Now I really know what's going on. This is why I don't talk to Momma much. What the hell does that mean?

"What about the tunnel?" Momma asks. "You didn't touch it, did you?"

"I wanted to. I almost did. But I was afraid of disappearing. I thought that I would vanish like a stain in the wash. I just couldn't do it."

"Karina, you won't vanish. You will absorb," she says.

"Maybe, but it didn't feel like that," I say.

"If that's the case, it may be just as well you didn't touch it," she says. "Remember, your thoughts become the reality."

Reality, as if I know what that word even means right now.

"I'm going for a run. I'm not very hungry yet. I'm going to jog by the tower."

"Okay, but try to come back for dinner. Gramma is making lemon chicken with corn relish and fresh herbed salsa."

I've decided not to jog in the park, even though I'm pretty sure Mary has an angel or two watching over me. I'm going to run in the woods, behind the water tower. No one ever goes there. Jake and I used to spend whole afternoons climbing the tower and having picnics in the pines. Way back when.

The woods here are hilly. Large rocks are embedded in the Earth. I like being near them. They remind me of the stones in the purple dream. I never noticed before, but these rocks have an energy too.

I'm pacing myself up the hill toward the tower. My breath becomes labored sooner than I thought it would. I suppose I should join the gym like everyone else and get myself in shape, but the thought of living that kind of life still leaves a flat taste in my mouth. I force myself to run to the top. I lay down and rest in a spot I have lain in with Jake, and close my eyes to dream.

I must have fallen asleep, because it's starting to get dark. I jog around the tower once and head back down. Not much of the evening light makes it through the pine trees, but I know these woods by heart. I pick up my pace and run faster down the rocks, letting gravity pull me into it. I feel like I'm back inside a tunnel. Coming around a corner, I forget a rock I should have remembered and trip, twisting my ankle and hitting my head against a fallen tree.

"Shit." My head really hurts and so does my ankle. The woods seem really dark. I wonder if I was out for a while. I touch my ankle and it feels pretty swollen. This is great, just great. I try to stand on my ankle, but it gives under me. I'm really dizzy. I know that I shouldn't fall asleep, but it's hard to stay awake.

I must have gone to sleep again, because it's really cold now. What's that? There's a crackling sound, like twigs being broken. It's probably a squirrel, or a skunk, or Anne's rapist. I should've stayed asleep.

There's a beam, from a flashlight. Maybe someone's looking for me. Did I tell Momma where I was going? I can't remember. I usually don't. Kids come up here at night to party. Could be just a couple of kids who are drunk, maybe even high on drugs. Don't go there, Karina.

The light comes closer, but I still can't see who's holding it. I flew off to the side of the trail when I fell. Maybe if I don't move they won't see me. On the other hand, I can't stay here like this. I'll get hypothermia, or something, and die.

I can see the shadow of a figure on the trail. He's a big guy. The light is pointing away from him but I can tell now that it's Jake. Thank God, and not. I'm glad it's someone I know, but this is a pretty humbling moment. After all the times I told him I didn't need him anymore, that he was too protective. Maybe I should just stay here and hope for another rescuer. But my ankle complains, and my head. Time to eat some humble pie.

"Jake." The word comes out low, almost a whisper. Still, my head hurts from the effort.

The light moves over the ground till it finds where I lay.

"Karina!" Jake sprints to me. "Is anything broken?"

"My ankle, maybe."

He lifts my head and I can see the concern in his face. His hands are trembling.

"Ouch," I say. "I hit my head."

He takes off his jacket and wraps it around me.

"Just don't talk." He runs his lips softly across my forehead, as if willing me to be okay. "I'll get you to the hospital."

"No, not the hospital. Take me home."

"Karina, your ankle is broken and you probably have a concussion." I hear frustration creep into his voice.

"But I can't afford it. And I don't have any insurance."

"What are you talking about? You're on my insurance."

"I thought you had to take me off when we got divorced." His eyes widen. He's looking at me like I just stabbed him in the chest.

"You must've hit your head pretty hard, Karina. We're separated, but we're not divorced. Unless you filed the papers when I wasn't looking, we're not even close to it."

Now my head is really spinning. He's right. It's probably better if I don't talk right now.

In the emergency room they set my ankle and x-rayed my head. I must be okay, because they gave me some really good drugs. They're keeping me in the hospital. For observation, they say. Just for one night, most likely.

"Jake, go home and get some sleep," I say.

"I can sleep here. I told your mother I'd stay. She'll be over in the morning. I figured you wouldn't want to deal with her right now, so I said you'd be fine. I hope I wasn't lying."

"Thanks. But right now I just want to rest. You really don't have to stay. I'll be all right."

"I'm staying, Karina. I have that right. In spite of what you might wish, you're still my wife."

I don't know what to say. Don't know what he's talking about. If he didn't keep calling me Karina, I'd question my own name right now. I need to talk to Momma. Can't believe she didn't come. I know what she's thinking: That this will bring us together, but how can it when I don't even know where or when I stand in this relationship? Did the things that I remember not really happen? Did other things happen that I don't know about? Did I hit my head that hard? I look at Jake looking at me.

"Good night," I say.

"Sleep tight, Karina."

The sky is dark and I feel strangely light. My ankle? No. It seems to be okay. Hmm. Must be the drugs they gave me. I'm floating in a sea of stars.

Dreaming. Yes. I must be dreaming. Weird, though. My dreams aren't usually this real. Well, except the Goddess dreams.

"I'm happy to see you made it."

"Mary? What are you doing here? I mean, I'm glad to see you, but..."

"The question might better be, do you know why you're here?"

"Where is here?" I ask.

"That's what I thought. You've come back to dark blue. Apparently you had some unfinished business here. Do you know what it was?"

"No. Does it have anything to do with my head, and the fact that I can't remember still being married to Jake?"

"It very well could. Do you remember the last thing I said to you before you left here?" Mary asks.

"No."

"I said, 'just try to remember what happened here, pay attention to what happens there, and learn from it all.'"

"Try to remember what happened here. That would be the thing with the lawyer. The papers I didn't file, but how does that translate into my real life?"

"Your real life?"

"Yes, you know, my Earth life."

"Is that what you think? That the rest of your existence isn't real?"

"Well, I don't think it's nonexistent. I mean, I know that it's something. I just thought that it was not a part of reality."

"What is reality?" she asks.

"Reality is, you know, what I experience."

"And didn't you experience the incident with the lawyer?"

"Yeah, but in the dream," I say.

"Think back, Karina. Remember I told you that I was going to give you a very special tour of the mechanics of karma?"

"Yes, I remember that."

"In order for you to truly learn karma, you had to experience it in a way you could understand, in your 'normal dimension.'"

"So that was real? But how can you change time around like that?" I ask.

She is laughing now. "Time fluctuates all on its own, Karina. That was the easy part. Getting you to see and participate in it, that was more difficult."

"But then you're saying we never really did get divorced? And if I want to be divorced I have to do it all over again?"

"Yes. That's a decision you have yet to make. For now, you must live with your most recent decision."

"I don't understand. What happened to the time when we were divorced? And all those days when I journeyed, those must have still happened or I wouldn't be here now."

"You're getting ahead of yourself, Karina. The lesson here is about decisions and consequences. I must go now, but remember what I said."

"Wait. Wait. I need to know more..."

"Wake up, Karina." Jake is shaking me. "You were shouting in your sleep."

"I was? What did I say?"

"Wait, wait. I need to know more."

"Is that all?" I ask.

"That's all I heard. I was sleeping before that," he says.

"Oh God, I'm really disoriented."

"Do you want me to get you a doctor?"

"No, I'll be all right. Please don't call the doctor," I say.

"Whatever you say," He says, looking as though he doesn't believe a word I say.

"You know I never did thank you for finding me in the woods. I probably would have died if you hadn't come by when you did."

"Come by? Is that what you think? I just happened to be in the neighborhood, and since you were so close to death, I thought I'd drop in and see if I could help. Is that it, Karina? Do you think that's how it happened?"

"That's not what I meant. I was just saying thank you and you turn it into an ugly scene, like I'm some kind of criminal who did this to you on purpose. Why can't you just say 'your welcome,' like the rest of the world?"

"Right. That's what every other man on Earth would have done if he'd spent hours looking for his wife in the dark of the woods. How many times have I warned you about jogging alone, Karina. I can't talk to you now, or I'll say something I'll regret. I'm going for a cup of coffee. I'm sure you'll be all right without me."

God, men can be so obtuse. What is it about their insensitive souls that make everything I say have to be couched in sensitivity? I really don't get it.

But I can't think about it any more. It makes my head pound. And I'm so tired already. Too tired to think like that.

My journal, I should write in my journal, but I know I can't. Maybe Momma will still keep hers.

June 21

Guide's Journal, Twelfth Entry

Karina had the most wonderful journey today. She learned about the Spirit's true form, and Jake was there with her. Karina listened to her innermost self, fought her wild beast, and followed her heart into the place where Spirits soar. I watched her burdens falling away from her as she began to focus more and more on her goal of finding the center of power. But she couldn't hold that knowledge into and through the tunnel. I hope she finds a way to resolve the polarizing conflict inside herself. Her life will be much easier once she does.

After the journey, she left here and hurt herself badly, which I don't understand. She is not transferring her lessons into her Earthly life very well. Jake found her. He says she'll be okay. I've lit a candle, and I'm praying to Mary for her safety and for Jake's patience. Blessed be.

Chapter Twelve - Black and White
Cause and Effect

The drone of the intercom, "Paging Doctor Triecsh," awakens me.

I open my eyes to see Momma's face hovering over me. She looks a little pale.

"How are you feeling?" she asks.

"Like someone ran over me with a truck. You don't look so good, either."

"I'm fine. I just didn't get much sleep last night," Momma says.

"I'm sorry, Momma. I'm sure you were worrying about me. I just...fell. And hit my head. I didn't see that rock."

"It's all right, Karina. You don't have to apologize to me. Although I'm not sure Jake feels the same way."

"Where is he?"

"He had to go. What did you say to him? " Momma asks.

"Who knows. No matter what I said it would have been wrong."

"Well, he was just very worried about you. He left work as soon as I called to go and find you. He was pretty shook up when he called from the hospital, although he tried not to show it."

"Why does he have to do that?" I ask. "Why does he have to hide it? How am I supposed to know what he's thinking?"

"Well," she says. "The fact that he came after you should have said something. With the way your relationship is, he certainly didn't have to."

"I'm glad you said that, because I need to know. Exactly how is our relationship? The last thing I remember, we were divorced and now we're still married."

"Yes. Well, that's a little tricky," she says.

"Tricky? This has gone way past illusion, Momma. My life has been altered here. What am I supposed to do with that?"

"What's important here is that you have a second chance at this relationship, if you want it," she says.

"Why does everyone keep saying that? How can I know if I want it, when I can't even get near the man, emotionally?"

"If you ask that question at the right time, the answer will come," she says. "Now you rest. I brought the Crystal Goddess with me. She's not just for journeying, you know. She's also a great healer."

Momma places the Goddess on my belly. I close my eyes and feel her energy radiating through me. I try to remember things that have happened, hoping to find the pieces that help to make sense of it all. Strange things come into my head. Pictures of places I've been to, childhood songs, meditations I learned. Which one am I up to? Oh yes, black and white.

"You follow a cycle
that no eyes do see,
each piece being captured
quite separately.

Once yesterday's dew
now today's sunrise,
your mysteries cloud
the clearing skies.

Your passionate winds
and endless cries
find spaces to whisper
and revitalize

Inside the darkness
that rests in the light,

show me that moment
when day becomes night."

I am in a courtyard. The ground is a large black and white chessboard. There are statues of kings and queens, knights on horses, bishops, and many, many pawns. It's early morning. The Sun is just cresting the top of the castle. Beams of light find the holes reserved for muskets in case of attack. A ray of light falls at my feet. A woman dressed in a flowing white robe walks into the light to greet me. She's holding two ebony chalices. She passes me one.

Smiling broadly, she holds hers high and says, "To thy quest."

"To my quest. Wait..."

I am in a room where the windows are draped with heavy black curtains. The thick pile carpet is white as snow. So is the cushy leather sofa. There are cast iron statues and black lacquered tables scattered throughout. A woman dressed in black is sitting on a pillow at one end of a coffee table. She is shuffling cards and humming a sad, soft tune. I know the melody, but not the name. She looks up and nods for me to join her. She lights the white candle in the middle of the table.

She passes the cards to me. I know what to do. Momma has always used Tarot cards. I've watched her read for other people. She sometimes reads for me, although I rarely ask.

The woman is young, but she has the confidence of someone who is familiar with the cards. Not everyone who holds the cards can use them well.

"Wait a minute. What happened to the bath? I can't be here without the bath can I?"

"The bath is just a catalyst," she says. "A tool to help put you in the dreaming frame of mind. It seems you didn't need it."

"It seems so," I say. "What's your name?"

"Mimosha," she says.

Mimosha looks at the cards and then looks at me. The room smells of opium. I breathe deeply.

"All right," I say. Picking up the deck, and holding it in my left hand, I ask the question silently to the deck. "What is this journey telling me about my future, and how does Jake fit into it?" Mimosha will read the Tarot's answers, without knowing the question.

"You may cut it," she says. I cut the deck.

She turns over the card I have cut. It is the significator: The card that characterizes the background of my question.

"The Tower," she says. It's a picture of a tall building on fire. At the top of the building is a crown that has just been blown off by a bolt of lightning. Two people are falling from the burning tower.

"The message here, as with most cards, is symbolic." Mimosha explains. "The crowned tower represents the materialization of spiritual matters. The lightning and the fire are the spirit's response to being enclosed. The people, twisting while falling, represent the downward spiral of false beliefs. For you this card is important because it represents a dilemma between the material and spiritual worlds. You are drawn to one and in need of the other. The falling people are symbolic of relationships which have lost their connections in spiritual matters, at least in the material world."

Mimosha turns over another card. She places it over the first card. It is the cover card: The card that covers what is significant in my question. It may be hiding or simply influencing the subject of my question.

"The Five of Cups." The picture is a dark, cloaked figure looking sideways. He is looking at three cups lying on their sides. Behind him are two cups standing upright. There is a bridge in the background, leading to a small building.

"This is a card of loss, but something remains. Some say it is the card of a frustrated marriage. For you, Karina, I see it as a man who has drunk your life, but now mourns the loss of it. Some remains, hidden behind him. Perhaps something in his past has preserved this portion. At any rate, the bridge is available to lead him and you, the cups, to the house on the other side. That this will happen is uncertain, however, because he must turn around first, to find what he has lost."

Mimosha turns over the third card. The crossing card: It crosses the question and the cover card. It can be a helping card to the cover or an objection obstacle.

"The Ten of Swords." It is a figure, male or female, I'm not sure, lying in a barren land, under a dark sky, pierced in the back by ten swords.

"This is a card of pain, sadness and desolation. For you, Karina, it is also a card of loneliness. There is a part of you that revels in this card because you understand this kind of pain. You understand desertion and tears. As long as you can be the victim of the swords, you do not have to deal with the spiritual dualism of the tower or the conflict of the cloaked figure, the Five of Cups. You use this pain to justify your hiding place."

Boy, she doesn't waste any time mincing words.

"Am I on the right track here, Karina?" Mimosha asks. Although I have a feeling that she knows she is.

"You can continue," I say. If I weren't afraid of looking like a coward, I'd ask if she wouldn't mind going a little easier on the straight talk.

She turns over the next card, placing it in the future trends position. This card shows the direction I am heading, unless I change course by my actions.

Until this point, the cards were all in one pile. The second on top of the first, covering it and the third laid perpendicular over them, forming a cross. I'm relieved to see that she is using the "cross" layout, one that I recognize. There are eleven cards used in the basic cross layout. The cards are placed horizontally and vertically to form a cross. The remaining cards are set off to the side, each in a particular spot representing its relationship to the other cards.

"The Eight of Swords." Again with the swords! The picture shows a woman bound and blindfolded, with eight swords around her. She's standing above a trickle of water. In the background there is more water and a castle up on a hill. The bonds are loose, and the swords are stuck in the mud around her.

"This is a card of conflict and crisis, but not permanent bondage." Mimosha says. "For you, Karina, this card shows the future if you continue to live blindfolded to your true goals and purposes in life. The bondage comes from a relationship, perhaps with the cloaked figure, perhaps with a relative, or perhaps with yourself. Only you can know this. In any event, you could easily use the water to free yourself. The water being symbolic of the spiritual world. The castle awaits you, if you choose to be free."

Mimosha turns over a fifth card. She places it in the foundation position. The foundation card represents the basis for the situation found in the significator card. It's the causation of the first three cards and the root of what is leading to the fourth card, future trends card.

"The Hermit." It's a picture of a hooded man holding a lantern and a staff, standing on top of a mountain. The lantern is lit and the hermit is looking down.

"The Hermit," Mimosha says, "is often a card of attainment, having reached the heights of enlightenment, but having done it alone. For you, Karina, in this position, and laying with these other cards, I read the hermit as a soul desiring enlightenment, but seeking isolation. Looking down upon those who might assist you in your search, you carry a lantern that no one will see, unless you find the strength to go down and share it with them.

"Working with other people is not always a bad thing, Karina." Mimosha smiles for the first time since the reading began. She looks older when she smiles, much older than I remember her looking a half-hour ago. Maybe the lighting was different.

Mimosha turns over the sixth card. We are halfway through the reading. It is the immediate future card. It usually suggests something that is already beginning to happen.

"The Lovers." The sun is shining and an angel is holding her arms and wings out, surrounding the male and female standing naked before her. The tree of life and the tree of good and evil are behind them.

"The Lovers. The card of human love, blessed by heavenly forces. This is a card of innocence, of a time before material desires. The man and the woman are not yet touching, but clearly belong to one another. For you, Karina, this card is a good omen. It means that there is still enough purity in the love you share with another that love can be recovered. To reach this, however, you must return to a place of spiritual youth."

"How do I find spiritual youth?" I ask.

"You seek it," she says.

Does she think I'm daft? I meant, where do you seek it? But the tone of her voice was so aloof that I don't dare pursue it with her. Maybe she can't read cards and converse at the same time. Or maybe my question just annoyed her.

Mimosha turns over the seventh card: The card of the immediate past. This card represents a situation just finished. The immediate past is tied to the immediate future card.

"The Knight of Cups." The picture shows a graceful knight riding a horse. He's wearing a helmet with wings on the back and is holding a cup in front of himself.

"The Knight of Cups is a dreamer, but does not have good side vision, due to the constraints of his helmet. For you, Karina, this means that someone has found your cup, and is carrying it, somewhat blindly, toward an unknown destination. The rider is wearing armor, but is not war-like. He is trying to serve you, although you may not have recognized it as such."

Mimosha is good. I can't believe how closely what she sees follows my life, with a little imagination, though not too much. Looking at her again, I'm astonished at the change in her. The lighting couldn't have been that bad. She looks like a woman seventy or eighty years old.

"Are you all right, Mimosha?" I ask her.

"I am fine."

"But, a while ago you looked so young and now you look so old," I say.

"What is age, but a wrinkle in the face of time? A wrinkle is but a fold that can be unfolded and refolded as the need suits. You have experienced this, have you not?"

"Well, yes, but I don't really understand it."

"What's to understand? Reality is a creation of thought. We create and re-create according to our needs of the moment. It is simply living without material constraint. Which, if I am reading correctly, may be something you have to look forward to."

Mimosha turns over the eighth card: The self-card. This card shows the self or a part of the self that it's important to acknowledge at the point in time of this reading.

"The Fool." The picture is of a young, elaborately dressed figure who has walked gaily toward the edge of a precipice. She is high in the mountains, carrying a wand and a rose and looking up into the heavens. Her little doggy is bounding at her heels. The sun is shining in the background.

"The Fool." Mimosha says. "This card represents intelligence, dreams and travels for a creature not of this world. She is the spirit in search of experience. For you, Karina, it represents the person inside you who wants to stop hiding behind the distrust and skepticism that are plaguing your life and keeping you from experiencing it fully. It is telling you to enjoy more and dream more."

"Is it saying that I want to be like the fool, or I am like the fool?" I ask.

"It is saying that the part of you that is the fool wants to come out," she says.

Mimosha looks at me, and then turns the ninth card. After this, there are only two more cards to go. I suppose it's too late to stop now. It is the card of family and friends. This card refers to the people or the environment surrounding me, and to those surrounding the situation of my question.

"The King of Wands". The picture is of a king on his throne, holding a flowering wand. Lions and lizards are etched on his throne. His posture is straight, tall and noble.

"The King of Wands." Mimosha looks pleased. "This card represents a dark, animated, impassioned man. His crown is lined with a cap of maintenance. He is an upright, countryman. He is honest and conscientious and usually married. For you, Karina, this represents an honest man working in your life, trying to provide you with a security you need."

Mimosha looks into my eyes. My guess is she is trying to see whether I grasp the direction that this is all taking.

"Do you know who this man is?" she asks.

"It's not like I have that many men in my life," I say, forcing myself to hold her gaze. As I watch her, I see a change in her face. The wrinkles begin to soften and fade.

"You're becoming younger again," I say.

"As you wish," she says. "Shall we continue?"

"We've come this far. I might as well know the end."

Mimosha turns the tenth card. This is the hopes and fears card. The one you don't really want to see. Sometimes what you hope for most is also what you fear the most. It's commonly thought that, in this card, you will find that to be true.

"The Page of Swords." The picture is of a figure holding an upright sword. He walks on rugged terrain. There are dark clouds around him and birds flying high in the sky above him.

"The Page of Swords is a card of vigilance." Mimosha says. "The Page is strong and alert. He upholds the authority of the law, and is always on the lookout for spies and evil. For you, Karina, the card represents a desire to be protected and the fear of being crushed."

How did she know that? The eleventh card is the last. The outcome card. I'm really not sure that I want to see it, or want her to interpret it. She's uncanny with her observations. Momma was never this good. But then again, Momma wasn't in a dream, or maybe she was. I realize now that there is much more to Momma than meets the eye.

Without asking, she turns over the final card. It's The High Priestess. The picture is of a woman with a moon crown on her head and a crescent at her feet. She's seated between a black and a white pillar. Her robes are soft and full. She wears a cross at her breast and holds a scroll of the Torah.

"The High Priestess." Mimosha looks impressed. And very young again. "She represents the merging of the houses of God and man. A spiritual bride and mother, hers is the second marriage to the Prince who is no longer of this world. She is the bright reflection of the One Supernatural Mother. Mystically, she is the spiritual bride of the lawman. He brings justice and she gives it meaning.

"If you follow the path, being careful of the pitfalls you have seen, this card can be you, Karina. You are privy to special knowledge that you must learn how to share. But first, you must remove what is dulling the reflecting light."

Mimosha leans back in her chair and takes a deep breath. I follow her lead.

"It was a good reading," she says. "Don't you think so, Karina?"

"Amazing."

"Was your question answered?" she asks.

"In a little more detail than I might have liked, but yes. I got what I needed to know."

"You will do well with this knowledge, Karina. Take care to be mindful of what you have learned. You must get back now. Be good to yourself, and I'm sure that I will see you again."

The room begins to close into a swirling pattern of black and white. The black and white form stripes, moving very slowly, in a dizzying pattern. I can feel life in the pattern, in the stripes themselves. They feel like animals, zebras, running together in a herd. They are all of them moving together with a rhythm born of a lifetime of breathing each other's air, of watching out for one another when the lions and leopards come, moving in synch when another shifts. I feel the value of their ability to sense each other, to let go of what each individual is doing in the moment and bend to the stronger momentum of the herd. They don't care much about a momentary need. They move willingly with the energy that leads to safety.

The zebras are galloping in a circle around me. I am in the middle, a zebra alone. There is a lion in the center of the circle with me. He is watching the herd run, but cannot focus on a prey. He sees me.

I look at him closely. He definitely looks hungry. I know I should run to the safety of the group. That I should let myself join the flow of their circle dance, but I'm stuck holding onto myself. I feel myself trying to suck all my energy in, to hold it tight inside, like a bomb holds its power, wired with the potential of explosion.

The lion begins to walk slowly toward me. He's in no hurry. He can tell that I'm frightened and stuck to this spot, like an old man stuck in the grip of loyalty to a worn out politics.

The thought, "why can't I move? Why can't I move," is running over and over on the surface of my brain. Then I realize that I can. Yes, I can run. I don't have to hold onto this frightening energy. I don't have to stand here and fight this battle in my mind.

"Life is a process, Karina," I hear a voice in my head say. "Which implies that you must proceed. Go forward. Go with the flow. Let loose the reins."

"All right, all right," I say. I turn and bolt for the circle of zebras forming the wall. The wall parts. As easily as rainwater finding a home in the stream, I merge with the herd.

The lion is standing by the edge of the wall, dumbfounded. The circle speeds up. I'm sure we must look like one big, gray wall to him. To him, looking on, we are one solid mass, but to us inside, we are each other and ourselves. Safe in the circle, the stream that flows down the path of least resistance, we are riding the wave of the safety of the universe. And it feels really good.

The circle begins to form a funnel. As the momentum gets faster, the circle gets smaller, until we are a tiny ring, with a bright light in the center. I move into the light and follow it to my waiting body, lying on a sterile hospital bed, the statue still in my hands.

"Karina," Momma is saying. "Karina, the doctor is here to see you."

Without too much trouble I convince the doctor that I am well enough to go home. Auntie Connie arrived while I was dreaming. Together, she and Momma take me back home to where a warm meal and Gramma are waiting.

Drifting off to sleep in the comfort of my own bed, I can hear Auntie Connie's voice saying to Gramma, "Yes, She really journeyed, right there in the hospital."

"I've always said there was something special about that girl," Gramma says.

✤ ✤ ✤

June 22

Twelfth Journey: Black and White

    I met a woman who reads the Tarot cards. Her name was Mimosha. My question: what is this journey telling me about my future, and how does Jake fit into it?

    As always, the cards showed the direction I was heading, but left me with a choice. It seems I have some pretty basic insecurities. I want to be loved, but am afraid of being left; want to be protected, but don't want to be controlled; want to live in the spiritual world, but don't want to give up the comforts of the material. In other words, I want the prize, but don't want to risk losing by playing the game. Jake, it seems, is meant to be my lover, my protector, and probably my husband.

    Strange, but watching the cards unfold, seeing the lover, the king, the page, I saw a different view of Jake. I saw him as a person with his own weaknesses to overcome. I felt sorry for him standing there with three empty cups. I don't know. Maybe I've misjudged him. I've certainly misjudged myself. The cards believe I can achieve something special. Maybe I can. I finally touched the tunnel wall. It was awesome, like going home to someplace you've never been, but always knew was there. Tomorrow is my

last journey day. I'm going to go into the wall again--
if I can. K.

June 22

Guide's Journal, Twelfth Entry

Karina was way ahead of me on this journey. She was almost finished with it before I realized that she wasn't simply sleeping. By the time I joined her, Mimosha was on the final card. The outcome card predicted an honorable future for her. High Priestess, was the card. Karina has much more potential than she uses, probably because she is afraid to be great. She knows that comes with a price. I'm not sure that she sees herself as worthy of happiness. She is very worthy; and I'm going to tell her so. Blessed be.

The phone wakes me up.

"Hello."

"Hi, Karina. How ya feeling?"

"I'm all right. The ankle is a little sore, but my head isn't too bad."

There is a long silence.

"Well, that's all I really called for," Jake says. "I just wanted to make sure you were all right."

"Momma told me how quickly you came to find me. I'm sorry if I seemed ungrateful. I wasn't thinking too clearly."

"That's all right, Karina," he says. "I should have been more patient. It's just that you drive me so crazy with your indifference."

"My indifference? That's pretty ironic." I say.

"How's that?"

"Because what bothers me most about our relationship is that you don't seem to see me as a person anymore. You see me as some...I don't know, some item that needs protection," I say.

"I know. I seem to have gotten really caught up in the mechanics of living in a policeman's world. I got a pretty rude awakening to that last night."

"How do you mean?" I ask.

"Well, I had this dream. It was so real, Karina. I can't tell you how real it was."

"A dream? Would you tell me about it?" I ask.

"Well, there was this lady with these cards. Tarot Cards, you know, like your mother's. Anyway, she did this thing where she kept flipping the cards over and telling me this story of things in my life. She - well, the cards said that the way I was acting was hurting our relationship."

"So, in your dream, this lady was reading the cards for you?"

"Yeah," he says.

"Was anyone else in the room?"

"No. Just her and me."

"What was her name? Do you remember?" I ask.

"Her name? Why? Do you think you might know her?" he's laughing now. "It was something like a drink. Mimosa?"

"Mimosha?" I ask.

"Yes. That's it. Oh my God, you do know her!" he says.

"No, well, it's just that I had the same dream. Only she was reading for me."

"This is pretty creepy," he says. "Does this have something to do with your mother?"

"I don't know about Momma, but it's connected to the journey."

"Are you still doing that?" His tone of voice has changed now, but not in the way I expected it to. It sounds hushed.

"Yes," I say.

"When does it end?"

"Tonight. Tonight is my last trip into the Crystal Goddess's world. At least it completes this journey."

"You know I've been cynical about all this magic stuff, but the card lady reminded me of something I had forgotten," he says.

"What was that?"

"That I once believed in magic. As a boy, I ate up the stories of King Arthur and his Knights of the Round Table, and especially Merlin. I loved all that wizardry. It made life seem bigger."

"Life is bigger, Jake."

"Yeah. It's pretty awesome. Karina, I'd really like to see you. I think we need to talk some more."

"Yeah. Me too." I say.

"I mean," Jake says, "I know that just my saying 'I'm sorry' doesn't take away the years of hurt and neglect. And your saying it wouldn't make me feel any less rejected either, but I think we can work on it. Can't we?"

His voice sounds soft and tender, and I wish that he were here right now. Moments like this don't come too often. And their intentions last even less often. We've kissed and made up before. Still, maybe this time is different. He did have the dream.

"Can't we?" he asks again.

"Yes. We can work on it, but not until later tonight. I still have the journey to finish. I'll call you."

"All right." he says. "And Karina?"

"Yeah?"

"Be careful."

"Of course," I say.

Chapter Thirteen - The Rainbow Journey's End

Momma is preparing my final bath, and I'm almost sorry to see this journey end, although I think that, in a way, it never really does. Still, I'll miss Momma drawing the water and chanting those primordial sounding mantras while I rhyme myself off into otherworldly dreams. Even though we don't share our feelings much, I feel closer to her during the preparation, even during the dreaming than I have ever felt before. As I watch her now, so focused on the simplicity of her actions and her intentions behind them, the depth of her beauty awes me.

"Karina, I've been trying to think of how to explain tonight's journey to you, how to prepare you for it," Momma says. The closest I can come is to say that it's like a final exam of the lessons you've learned."

I feel a tightening in my gut, like someone just punched me.

"Exam? No one said there would be an exam. Was I supposed to be memorizing this? Why didn't you say something earlier? You know I'm terrible at tests."

"Did I say exam? No, I meant more like a report card."

"Report card? That's worse. It's like I've already taken the test without knowing it. How could you let this happen?"

"Relax, Karina. I'm sure you did just fine. Just fine." Momma says.

"Momma, you know I hate that word "fine." It sounds like, 'well, you tried your best, Dear, even if you did fail.' I'm not going dreaming just for the humiliation of a report card. Anyway, what gives anyone the right to grade me on anything?"

"Karina, you have to finish the journey. There's a large piece still missing. You have to find it and put it in place. I only told you this so that you'd be prepared. Now I see that I shouldn't have."

"Should or shouldn't isn't the point. What if I failed?"

"Listen to me, Karina. This last dream is very important. You will just have to trust me."

Trust is something I still don't do too well. Momma has got me through the journeying all right so far. A couple of times I wasn't so sure, but I know now that the whole experience has made me stronger.

"I hope you're right," I say. "I would like to finish this, but now you've scared me."

"Don't worry about anything. Just go and learn what you're meant to learn," Momma says.

I look to see if she will let her eyes meet mine. She does, and holds them for a moment. I decide I can trust her. At least I know her intentions are true.

"I'm assuming you touched the tunnel in your last dream?" Momma says.

I'm trying to read her. Does she want a dissertation, or just confirmation? Keep it simple, I decide.

"Yes, I did."

"Try to do it again," she says. "And one more thing."

Oh no. It's got to be big. One more thing that she has saved until this point in time cannot be good.

"No matter how this turns out, I love you; and I'm very proud of you," she says.

You could knock me over with an incense stick. I can't remember the last time that Momma said that she loved me. I never, ever thought she'd be proud of me.

"I love you too, Momma."

Momma leaves me to my bath.

When I see her again in the journey room, it is a as though she was always gentle and kind. I wonder which of us has changed.

She begins to hum. And I begin my rhyme to the rainbow of colors:

"When Red finds a passion
that she cannot hold
and Pink learns of love
more precious than gold,
When Orange finds a reason
to feed the unfed
and Peach with compassion
each moment is led,
When Yellow reaches into
the cells it has lost
And Sea Green brings home
respect at a cost,
When Green will awake
and atone for her sins
and Light Blue will solve
her problems within,
When Dark Blue finds solace
in choosing her way
and Purple lifts spirits
to dance as they pray,
Then Black and White
shall share their insight
and all the colors
will play 'till it's night."

    I am in a place straight out of a lucky charms commercial. Complete: The rainbow, the pot of gold, and the little leprechaun.

    "Top of the mornin' to ya," he says as he bows his tiny little body in half.

    He is so adorable it makes me smile. Well, maybe he's lucky.

"Come a wee bit closer, Lass. I've got something special for yee." He's dipping something into the pot that is holding the light at the rainbow's end.

"What is it?" I ask, leaning over. I can't help myself. I've always wanted to look into one of these.

He pulls out a ladle filled with a shimmering liquid.

"It's actually quite good," he says. "See, It won't hurt you." He takes a sip to prove it's not poisonous. "And a fine toast to your journey it be."

The twinkle in his eyes is enough to make me believe that I want whatever it is, regardless of taste or consequence. I take the ladle from him and watch as the liquid swirls in a spiral, turning in upon itself. It's really too pretty to drink, and too hypnotic not to.

"To my journey," I say, and up-end the ladle.

I am in a huge glass house, filled with mirrors. It's like the amusement park version, except that strategically placed prisms dramatically cut the sunlight. There's a line in front of me in which I see descending images of myself. I count twelve "me's," each in a different color. They are in the order of my journey. The first, the Karina covered in red light, is motioning me to come closer.

I step closer and she disappears. Now I am covered in red. I feel my temperature begin to rise, as I stand alone in the light.

An old man with white hair and a long white beard, dressed in a robe that looks like something a scribe would have worn, appears in front of me. He is holding a scroll and reading from the parchment.

"In adjudication to your indoctrination into the color red: We, the observation committee, hereby proclaim that your passion is pure. In light of this, you may go on."

The man disappears. That's it? He pronounces my passion is pure and I go on? I'm not sure if I like his style of report card. It's so…cryptic.

I'm faced again with an image of myself. Bathed in pink, she is motioning me to come near. As I step toward her, she disappears. I stand in the pink light and wait. Where did she go? Did I become her? The man with the white beard appears. He unrolls his scroll a bit further.

"In adjudication to your indoctrination into the color pink: We, the observation committee, hereby proclaim that your love is true and lasting. In light of this, you may go on."

Again, he disappears. Well, this isn't so bad, really. It's straight-forward. I can handle this.

Another "me" catches my eye. She's so real. It's like I'm really her. She is lit with orange. She motions me toward her. I reach out to see if I can touch her, but she disappears, leaving me to stand alone in her orange.

The scribe appears. He is so aloof. It's driving me crazy. He looks at me for a moment. What is he thinking? Did I fail this color? Of course I failed. I left it in a cramping fit of nerves and frustration.

White beard unrolls his scroll. "In adjudication to your indoctrination into the color orange: We, the observation committee, hereby proclaim that your balance, while teetering slightly, is sufficiently stable. You may go on."

Orange felt more like a full tilt to me, but I'll take the grade and be happy. Maybe there's a curve for this color. Chaos and control is not an easy study. Funny, I think of that dream now whenever I get too uptight.

I'm calling myself again. It's odd, but I feel like I'm both Karinas at once. Like, I know that I'm calling myself to come closer, and I know I'm stepping into my space. I'm peach this time. Shrouded in its soft, comforting light, I wait.

White beard appears. It might be my imagination, but I could swear he winces each time I think of him this way.

"Ahem," he says. He unrolls his scroll and reads. "In adjudication to your indoctrination into the color peach: we, the observation committee, proclaim that your compassion is genuine. In light of this, you may go on."

This is actually kind of nice. It almost seems like they like me, whoever they are. Is it really I, or just my actions? It's strange how as much as these Karina's actually feel like me, somehow there's a me that is separate from all of them. Even this me. I feel this separation almost as keenly as I felt the cohesion of the zebra herd.

My body, veiled in yellow, is beckoning me. I step into a light that feels like the sun done in watercolor. If they could bottle this color and give it to depressed people, I'm sure pharmaceutical stocks would drop over night, or rise, if the FDA classified it as a drug.

He appears again. I wonder where he goes.

"That is not important," he says. "What is important now is my proclamation. Or do you want to be here all night?"

"You speak," I say. "I was beginning to think you were a hologram."

"Indeed," he says. "If I may continue?"

I nod.

"In adjudication to your indoctrination into the color yellow: We, the observation committee, proclaim that your intellect is expanding. In light of this, you may go on."

"Wait a minute," I say. But he doesn't. Wow. I'll have to watch what I think around here. I guess everybody's in on the thought waves. My next self is gesturing me on. Washed in sea green, she looks almost wistful, whimsical and mystical. I want to be her. I step into the light and feel released from worries.

White beard comes quickly now. Maybe he was just waiting, before, to hear what I was thinking.

"All thoughts are freely given and freely received here. If one doesn't want to be heard, the polite thing to do is to remain silent," he says.

"I don't know how to do that," I say.

"Just stop the mind chatter," he says. "Limit your thoughts to your inner voices."

"I'll have to work on that," I say.

He smiles for the first time. "We have all had to work on something," he says. "Now, on to the business at hand."

I was so taken by the scribe and the setting before that I didn't notice the scrolls. This one is sea green. I wonder what they really say. I can't imagine that he has to unroll all that paper just to read a two-sentence verdict.

"In adjudication to your indoctrination into the color sea green: We, the observation committee, find your ability to observed and perceive most satisfactory. In light of this, you may go on."

I feel a little bit of pride in hearing him say this. Lately, I've noticed that I am more careful of my viewpoint. Although, frankly, I thought I'd learned something different in sea green.

He is back. "There is much to learn in each color, and we have judged you on all of it. The lesson most important to each person, however, carries the weight of the final ruling."

As quickly as he came, he is gone. "Thanks," I say, into the sea green air.

A Karina, seeped in the color of chlorophyll, is motioning with a gentle arm for me to come closer. I step into the lushness and take over her wavelength.

White beard appears. He unrolls his scroll. I wonder if this is really necessary, or if it's done purely for theatrics.

"It is necessarily done for theatrics," he says. "Now, I'd like to go on. You do want to find out whether you have passed the rainbow course sometime this century, do you not?"

"Yeah, but, if you don't mind my saying so, this is kind of an odd report card."

"Ahem." He says. Then he looks at me as though he is waiting for something.

"Has anyone ever told you that you're very impatient?" I ask. He continues to stare.

"Well, go on, then." I say.

"In adjudication of your indoctrination into the color green: we, the observation committee, find that your body has an acceptable awareness of sensitivity to the emotional, intellectual and spiritual experiences of this lifetime. Therefore, you may go on."

Sensitive, and all this time I thought I was crazy. Not true. I'm just sensitive.

"And, more importantly, aware of your sensitivity." He says.

"Hey, do you have a name?"

"Is that important to you?"

"Of course it's important. I have trouble talking to people whose names I don't know."

"No, you don't. But if it will help, my name is Mel."

"Why don't you just introduce yourself when you first meet someone. It would make things a lot nicer."

"Most people are not comfortable being on a first name basis with the pronouncer of their judgment. Particularly people who dress me as you have."

"Wait a minute. You came out here looking like that."

"At your request. Anyway, it's a fine costume. Wouldn't change it for the world. Now, if you would like to finish sometime in this lifetime, I suggest we move on. Even though, as you know, time is relative. Still, the suspense does build."

He disappears again. Momma always says I talk too much. Especially when I'm nervous, and it has just occurred to me that I am, in fact, very nervous.

I look up and see myself basking in the hue of teal. I, the teal me, am throwing my head in a backward beckoning motion.

"Yeah, I'm coming," I say to myself. Standing in the light of teal, I feel kind of new, fresh maybe. It's nice.

Mel is back. "Would you like a history lesson this time, or can we move on?" he asks.

"We can move on." I hope I don't lose points for blowing up Jake.

"Jake escaped, narrowly. But then you knew that. Anything else?" He sounds impatient.

"Sorry. No."

"Good." He unrolls his scroll a bit further. I notice that this one is teal. "In adjudication of your indoctrination into the color teal: We, the observation committee, find your vision far-reaching and your empathy for your host planet commendable. In light of this, you may go on."

"Can't you just tell me if I passed the whole thing?" I ask.

"I could, but then you wouldn't know what it was we liked or disliked about your scholarly endeavors. And, after all this effort, that would simply be a shame."

He's gone again. In another setting I think I could really like Mel. In this one, however, I'm having a challenge.

The image of myself cast in the blue of the sky is saying, "come closer." It's strange to hear myself speak to me. I step into the lightness of blue and wonder at the artistic perfection of choosing this color to paint the sky. Creators just have a knack for decoration, I guess.

Inspired by this thought, I look up at the ceiling. The mirrors and glass are so overwhelming down here that I hadn't even thought to look up. It's breathtaking. There is a huge crystal ball hanging from the center of a cathedral-style ceiling. It isn't completely round. The outside of the sphere is cut at angles that bend the light into separate wavelengths. Each of the journey colors is shooting out from one side of the crystal. Each me, below, stands in her color. Maybe I am the hologram. Now the ball is turning and the Karinas are shifting. Each of them is smiling or laughing with a slightly different expression than the others. They are on a carousel ride. As they turn, I feel a lifting in my belly, as though I am on the ride.

"What are you doing?" I ask.

Mel appears, scroll in hand. "You wanted a better view. We have provided one. Doesn't it please you?"

"Yes. It's lovely. But, I think that's enough for now," I say.

"As you wish," he says.

Mel begins to unroll the scroll and, without hesitating reads: "In adjudication of your indoctrination into the color sky blue: We, the observation committee, find your hypothesizing aptitude acute, and your assessment of your human world perceptive. In light of this, you may go on."

He's gone again. I guess he doesn't feel like chatting. I hope I didn't insult him by thinking I didn't like him in this setting. I actually forgot that he'd be listening. "Don't feel bad, Mel," I say to the air. "Most people find a way to annoy me."

"The last thing I can feel from this vantage point is bad," he says without materializing.

"Well, good. I'm glad to hear that, since it will probably take a few more decades of practice before I can learn to think without the internal dialogue."

"Centuries, more likely," he says.

"Hey, be nice, now. I haven't made fun of your scroll, as silly as it looks."

"We shall see who's silly when I have reached the end of it." He says.

Oh-oh, that sounded a little ominous. Maybe he's just a poor sport when it comes to jokes.

On cue, myself, draped in the dark blue of evening, waves me toward her. I step into her darkness. It surrounds me like a cloak of infinity.

Mel stands with a grave look on his face. This must be it: The place where I screwed up. Maybe you're not allowed to change things on the color journey. It could be one of those "Captain Kirk, non-interference" rules. But nobody told me that when I started. As a matter of fact, nobody gave me any rules, other than be careful and come out alive. Oh yeah, and learn the lessons.

"Very true." Mel says. "Still, how you learn the lessons and how you manage to stay alive are important."

"It wouldn't have hurt you all to tell me that in the first place. Or Momma, why didn't she tell me?"

"Rituals, by definition, must be carried out according to a specific plan. Your mother knows and honors the sovereignty of this rite. As for the committee,, it would be difficult for us to see how your true character is developing if we thought you might be putting on a performance for our benefit."

"Now, are you ready to continue?" Mel asks.

"Yes, ready as I'll ever be."

He unrolls the scroll. I hate that scroll.

"Hate is a very strong word," he says. Then, without waiting for my response: "In adjudication to your indoctrination into the color dark blue: We, the observation committee, find your grasp of karmic law lacking..."

"Oh, my God, I am going to fail."

"Did I say fail? And please don't interrupt my pronouncements. As I was saying...and your inability to make wise choices slightly irrational.

"The Virgin Mother, however, feels that you are striving to understand what is admittedly a difficult concept. And, because she has volunteered to work with you to complete this lesson, the committee has agreed to allow you to continue. In light of this, you may go on."

"Mary did that for me?"

"Yes. She did." He says.

"She's as compassionate as they say She is, isn't She?"

"You have no idea. And for some reason, she really likes you. You must be all right, because she is never wrong."

Mel disappears, leaving me to absorb the moment. Mary really likes me. I must be all right. Funny how you spend your whole life wondering if you really are all right. Then, in one flash, someone whom you know you can trust says you are, and everything is different. I'm really all right.

As I think this, my attention moves to an image of myself standing in the color purple. Does she know she's all right? By the look on her face, I'd say yes. Actually, I'd swear that is the same look I have on my face right now. Strange. She is signaling me into her color, and I go gladly.

A purple glaze fills the molecules in my space. It's purple, but bright and shining, reminding me of the bliss of the purple journey. Even if I do fail, it would be worth it for just those moments.

"Ahem," Mel says.

"Oh, I didn't see you there." I say. "Sorry."

"It's quite all right. Happens to everyone. It's the color." He says.

"I've always liked this color. Now I know why."

"Is that enough 'chit-chat', as your species likes to say. or shall we banter a little more until you're ready?"

"Has anyone ever told you that your social etiquette is lacking a few layers of really thick polish?"

"No. But then, as I said, most people do not find it necessary to converse with me quite so much as you do. Well, there was that one fellow. It would have been a long while ago in your time system. Socrates, I believe his name was." Mel looks at me sideways, with a strange little grin on his lips.

"Was that better?" he asks.

"Let's just get to it." I say. "You take all the joy out of small talk."

"Very well." Mel poises the scroll in that judicial position and then looks at me. "In adjudication to your indoctrination into the color purple: We, the observation committee, find your spiritual vibrations highly energized. Your skill in tapping into the great vault of mystical knowledge is sharpening. We have great hopes for your future progress. In light of this, you may go on."

"You have great hopes? Wow. I can't believe you said that. I mean, thanks."

"You're welcome." Mel says and fades away.

"You'll have to show me how you do that," I say.

"You won't get it in this lifetime. Transmogrification, maybe. But disappearing is a little different." He says. "But then again, I didn't give you great odds at the beginning of this journey, and look how well you've progressed. All the way through purple."

"All the way through purple? What about Black and White?"

There's no response.

It's weird talking to the air and having it talk back to you, and then not. It makes me wonder if he was ever real. I mean real, material. Like the images of me. I'm there, and then I'm not. But I'd swear I was solid to look at me.

"Then come here," says the image of me in black and white. It's odd how the light is split right down the middle of my face and body.

I take a step toward her. I fight the impulse to go into the light side. I know that the dark is just the light waiting to happen, but still, I prefer not to linger in that dormant period.

"Well," says Mel. "I may have to reassess my judgment of your lesson."

"Why? And don't you mean the committee will have to?" I ask.

"Because I didn't realize you understood the absolute of opposites. How one springs from the other. I'm quite impressed. And," he adds, "I am the committee."

"Thank you. But, if you are the committee, why don't you just say 'I proclaim,' instead of saying 'We?'" I ask.

"I prefer not to restrict myself to a singular personality. That is what you generally name. Is it not? The personality?"

"Yes, I suppose so." I say.

"And what if all the different personalities are not suited to the same name and actions as the one you think you project?" He asks.

"You're asking the wrong person," I say. "I've always had trouble trying to confine myself to one identity."

"Well, then you are in good company. And wise, although you don't know it," he says.

"Is that why each of the images of me in the colors looks slightly different?" I ask.

"What do you think?" he asks.

"I think they all feel like me, but none of them feel exactly the same."

"Which means?" he asks.

"Which, to me, means that all of the "Karinas" in the colors, all of the "dream Karinas," and all of the Karinas I feel on a daily basis are real, but none of them is the truest essence of me. That's something else, beyond all the actions and emotions."

"Very good, Karina."

"Does that mean I pass?"

"Yes, you pass. Good bye, Karina. For now. It's been an interesting trip. Give my best to your Mother. I will give your best to the rest of the coven. There will be a celebration for you on this side.

"And remember that Jake is also his truest essence. If I'm not mistaken, without all the clang of emotions, you two vibrated quite harmoniously."

I watch as Mel fades into the air. I picture Jake and a feeling of warmth comes over me.

"Good bye, old friend," I say. "Thanks for everything."

I look around one last time. The mirrors and glass begin to converge with the crystal ball on the ceiling. They are forming one large prism. Gathering light into its center and refracting it in a thousand different directions. Colors are splayed like peacock feathers, as far as my eye can see.

I can't help but remember the childhood lesson Momma taught me of the prism, and of the Ring of Fire. As I think of this, before my eyes a hole begins to burn into the air. Fire opens space from a point in the center. It spreads in a perfect circle, forming a door into what I'm sure is another dimension. Supported by the strength I feel in having completed my first full journey, I step through the fire.

Through the circle, I step into what must be heaven. The light is so bright it could blind, but it doesn't. I feel its energy. The walls of waves are vibrating so fast that they go past movement and back to calm.

I close my eyes and see myself in my purest form, a spirit. In this instant, I know that all the other images I hold of myself are illusions. The memories, the projections, the judgments of actions performed, all of these do not belong to me at all. They are props in the play of the conscious universe. They are like rides in an amusement park, like movies I've seen to entertain myself, like classes I've taken to learn things. They are experiences, but not the everlasting me. If I hold these experiences attached too tightly to my identity, then they eat up the energy of my life, a life that was meant to be a witness, not an emotional glutton.

The journey let me see that I was holding onto the images as if they were myself. There is no need for me to carry these as my self-image any longer. I release them back to their true owner. I let the universe absorb them.

I focus on the moment I now inhabit. If there is air here, it is so rarefied that it makes oxygen seem like a solid state. The energy and I are one. Yet I have not lost myself, as I feared I would. I am blissfully conscious of a perfect reality embracing me. I let the momentum of the spirit carry me toward a resting place...

I feel Momma before I see her. Her warmth kisses me. I open my eyes to see that she is glowing like the Goddess she is, and I know that I - my light also shines brightly. We embrace. There are no words for this moment, but giggles glide out of our bodies.

Gramma and Auntie Connie come to join us. We hold hands, encircling the Goddess statue, and bow our heads to thank her. At this intersection in my life's journey, I realize that the power that comes from these women and that which comes from the statue is the same.

And suddenly, in a breath of understanding, my knowing is filled with the inescapable realization that the lines that seem to divide one person from another, one spirit from another, are, in fact, arbitrary.

In allowing myself the liberty of participating in the cosmic merging, I realize, somewhat humbly, that this journey has brought me back to myself.

I know now that, in as much as I am any identity, I am the Rainbow Goddess.

I have anticipated dinner with Jake since the moment he mentioned it. Now I can hardly contain myself. I want so badly to say so much to him. I chose his favorite blue velvet dress to wear. I donned amethyst earrings and a large amethyst necklace in honor of the wonderful time we had in the purple dream-state. I am determined, this time, not to let my ego and my fears get the best of me. In the end, I have learned, there really is not much worth fighting about.

I am meeting Jake at his house, our house before I moved out. He is cooking the dinner. My guess is pasta. I don't care what it is, really, so long as it's peaceful.

Do I knock? Ring the doorbell, or just walk in? It feels very strange to be going back to our home.

"Hi, come on in." Jake meets me at the door with a kiss. I smile up at him, thankful for the break.

I look around. Everything seems the same as I left it, except for the missing furniture I took with me.

"Would you like a glass of wine?" he asks. "If I can find the corkscrew."

"Sure," I say, impressed that he has bought wine that requires a corkscrew.

We walk into the kitchen and I catch my breath. He has placed vases of roses on the countertops and the table. The room is alive with the scent of them. Candles are glowing, shallow tea candles, votives and tall purple sticks are casting a soft yellow light that warms the room and my heart.

Jake opens the bottle and pours two glasses.

"To you, Karina, and to your journey home," he says.

"Jake," I can hardly speak, the words come out a whisper. "I'm sorry for hurting you in so many ways," I say.

"No," he says. "I'm the one who should be sorry. Until last night, I didn't realize how much of a different person I'd become. I have not been the man you married and for that I am sorry. Will you forgive me?"

"How could I not?" I smile at him. "I have been forgiven so much myself."

"And we can start over?" he asks.

"Yes, we can start over." His hand reaches naturally over to gently push a stray lock of hair from my eyes.

"Are you terribly hungry now, or can we clean up before dinner?"

"What? Don't you like my dress?" I ask.

"Oh I like it," he says as his hand skims the velvet from my backside up to my zipper and start to ease it down. "I like it a lot." His lips drop gently to my neck and begin peppering me with angel softness. He dances me toward the bathroom where more candlelight and roses abound. He leaves my neck long enough to draw the bath water.

Jake smiles at me as he opens a bottle of rose bath oil and pours it in the tub.

"The girl at the store said it was the most romantic," he says.

He removes the rest of my dress and I help him with his clothes, kissing his chest and inhaling him deeply, I have missed that smell so much. A gurgle of laughter rises from his chest and I know that I have hit my mark.

We glide tenderly into the tub and connect through the silkiness of the softened water.

"AAhmm," I say. "I really think I'm going to like this new journey."

Would you like a sneak preview of our next release? Read on...

Hidden Voices

Chapter One

Gliding through dimensions, Ginger lighted between the place where molecules hang suspended in solid seeming masses and the vibrational world—where electrons flirt with form, but never settle down to marriage.

Ginger loved this space. It felt so much more real to her than the tangible Earth dimension where she tried hard to fit in, but rarely succeeded. And it was more welcoming than the many other dimensions she traveled in search of the inspiration; intuition or invisible guide spirit that would lead her successfully through the "Chalice Quest" her mother had bequeathed her.

Her mother, Ilssa, liked to refer to Ginger's life's mission as a "Chalice Quest," explaining that this was a wonderful image of the illusive, all-important, missing element that humans so loved to search for. Ilssa often read her young daughter tales of King Arthur. Because she knew she was meant to, Ginger strove to find connections between her life and his.

Ginger—in spite of her mother's best efforts—matured into a woman who was quite certain that the *Chalice*, the *Holy Grail* or any other goblet denoting victory would always remain tantalizingly out of reach. Still, because Ilssa had been so convinced that it was imperative, and that she was the only one who could espy it, Ginger had sworn to her mother that she would spend her life seeking the imaginary trophy.

She cursed herself, thinking it was too bad that she always kept her promises.

Sometimes Ginger let herself wonder at the serendipity of her life. She had lately, with the help of Dr. Jones, come to understand that there was something of a split personality in her.

"No more than most people have," Dr. Jones had assured her.

Although, on a logical basis, it explained some of the illogical decisions she made; and although it did give a rationale for the irrationally heavy sense of battle she often felt waging inside her over the stupidest of emotional issues, the idea of two consciousness' co-existing within her did not sit well.

Ginger knew that millenniums old Earth DNA reproduced itself in her body. Sometimes, when she let herself, she could feel her home planet's intelligence purring inside her. But, she also knew that she was half Merlite, and the consciousness of a civilization that had lived thousands of years without physical form often pulled her Spirit into the nether spaces and beyond.

That, she could understand. Being a Being of blended cultures was not easy, but it was thinkable. You could logic out when one culture influenced you more than another did. This thing about a split personality, a split mind, however, was different. There were no cultural rules to it. No history to follow and then say, "Ahh, the pressure of that particular influence explains this inclination."

No, she thought. Understanding the intricacies of her personality rift was not going to be easy. "Separating, dissecting and getting to know each of the personalities—the prescription Dr. Jones had given her—was different and much more difficult than understanding her heritage. Which is why, she knew, she frequently felt the need to escape to the astral world.

Somewhere around adolescence, Ginger had settled on the astral world as her dimension of choice. She loved the freedom of this world, the ease of its intensity. She loved being able to harmonize into the vibrant hymn of a lilac's scent; visualizing a destiny and instantly manifesting into it; being able to step through doors that were closed and to recognize aerial avenues that were open but shrouded from earthly sight. The astral world was Ginger's home. She had adopted it the way some people did a town. And she needed to protect it.

Ginger quickly learned that some pure humans frequented the astral plane, as did other spirits. She found the humans she met there to be more on her wavelength, literally. That had amused her. As time went by, she made all of her best friends while traveling the astral plane.

Getting to know the others and watching them fumble with silly barriers made Ginger aware that she had more control over her travels than most humans did. Meaning, she mused, that they occasionally needed her help.

That is why, when it came time to choose a career, Ginger became the Earth's first—to her knowledge—Astral Detective.

In time, everyone from wanna-be-psychics to the CIA had come to employ her services—services she tried very hard to keep discreet for fear they might interfere with her Chalice Quest.

Realizing that she had let herself wander off into "the minutia of the material," as her mother would say, Ginger gently brought her thoughts back to her "slip of silence," her focal point. She centered and then let go.

For a brief moment she was in the enchanted whirl of bliss. The pacifying hum of the astral atmosphere buoyed her. Life was Light.

Then she felt the shift. An energy entered into her world that made her shiver. Cold penetrated Ginger's consciousness.

A veil of darkness draped down on her.

"Go home," a rough and raspy voice spoke into her mind. "You cannot help them now. No one can."

Ginger felt herself brace to fend off the voice. It had a will and a tenacity she wasn't used to in human beings. The darkness receded as the anima behind the voice retreated.

Why had it said that? Ginger felt sure the voice had read her mind, had known what her reaction would be. Had it wanted to make her determined to stay? Or was she just imagining it?

The jolt of an insistent guilt reminded her that there was a specific reason why she'd come to the astral plane today. The last couple of days had been so hectic and confusing that Ginger felt out of touch with her instincts. Even so, she knew one thing for sure. She knew why she had come to the astral plane. She knew she had to find Mac.

"Mac," Ginger called into the void. "Mac, why won't you answer me?" Panic pricked painfully at the corners of her mind. "Oh, my God," she said into the aural void, "has he got you, too?"

Please visit our Web site at

www.moontress.com

We'd love to hear your comments!

Thank You for Joining our Journey!

Payable in U.S. funds only.   No cash/COD accepted.   Postage and Handling: U.S./Can. $3.00 for one book; $1.50 for each additional, not to exceed $9.00. For International P&H, please see our web site. We accept Visa, M.C., money orders & checks ($15.00 fee for each returned check).

Call 906-228-6181.

Or visit our web site @ www.moontress.com

Rainbow Goddess: A Journey Tale

ISBN 0-9701835-0-X

Moontress Press
P.O. Box 477
Marquette, MI 49855

Bill my: __Visa__MC____/____expires

Card# _____

Signature _____

Please allow 4-6 weeks for delivery
Foreign and Canadian Delivery 6-8 weeks

Bill to:

Name _____

Address _____ City _____

State/ZIP _____ Day Phone _____

Ship to:

Name _____ # of Books _____

Address _____ Book Subtotal $_____

City _____ Sales Tax $_____

State/ZIP _____ P & H $_____

Total

Encl./Charged $_____

This offer subject to change without notice.